DEGENERATION

AGE OF EXPANSION

DEGENERATION

THE GHOST SQUADRON BOOK 4

SARAH NOFFKE

MICHAEL ANDERLE

For Lydia. My greatest treasure in the universe.
-Sarah

To Family, Friends and
Those Who Love
To Read.
May We All Enjoy Grace
To Live the Life We Are
Called.
- Michael

Planet Sagano, Behemoth System

Heat blasted Eddie as he ducked under fallen trees, staying in a crouch as he sprinted through the burning jungle. The fire at his back was growing in intensity, even though the crews had been fighting it for days.

A loud crack jerked his attention overhead. The fire had overwhelmed a large stand of trees, that had fallen in on each other until the largest chose the direction they were going to fall. Eddie rolled to the side, dirt and ash raining down on him as the burning trees hit the ground exactly where he'd been.

He didn't pause, dashing forward to clear the next part of the conflagration. His vision blurred from his incredible speed, and his feet hardly felt as if they touched the soft ground before rising again.

Flames licked the side of a building, having jumped from nearby branches, but Eddie sped up the ladder to the house on stilts. Entering a burning building was one thing, but entering one that was held up by wooden poles in the middle of a forest fire was something else entirely. None of this seemed at all like a good idea.

Too bad he didn't have a choice.

Eddie opened the trap door at the top, which slammed over as he spilled into the jungle hut. As he scanned the room, smoke burned his eyes. The living space and kitchen were combined but there were some rooms at the back, so he ran in that direction while wiping tears from his eyes.

He kicked the first door open and searched the room, which was empty. The structure rocked, probably from the fire consuming the front of the house, which was where the next set of rooms was located.

Without hesitating, Eddie darted for the next room and rammed his shoulder into the door, ripping it off its hinges. He still wasn't used to his enhanced strength. After all, he'd only had this body for a short time. No one there either.

Eddie pivoted to the adjacent wall and shot his foot straight at the door. The interior was empty at first glance, and fire and smoke spilled through the open window. Eddie covered his face from the blaze and was about to head for the next room when something caught his eyes.

Between the wall and the bed on the far side of the room was a small boy.

Thank the fucking stars! Eddie thought, relief swelling in his chest. "Come on!" yelled Eddie, extending a hand to the kid, who was about four years old. The boy's large eyes stared at the intruding fire, and his face was swollen and red from the heat.

"It's okay! Come on, pal," Eddie urged him. He dashed

forward and scooped the kid into his arms, disregarding the intense heat on that side of the room. "Hold on to me."

The child clutched Eddie's neck tightly and wrapped his legs around the man's waist.

Eddie ducked as low as he could with the boy attached to him, and ran toward the ladder. He could hear the boy sobbing, although it was barely audible over the sound of the fire destroying the house. He wrapped one arm around the child's back and shielded his eyes from the smoke with his other hand.

"It's going to be all right," Eddie screamed over the crackling flames.

The boy vibrated with terror as Eddie carried him back to the trap door. The house rocked forward this time, and Eddie lost his footing and slid. The floor was at an angle now, and the stilts weren't going to remain upright much longer. Eddie realized that they were at the lowest point of the house, so if it fell they'd be crushed in the burning destruction.

Eddie threw their combined weight forward to make up the ground they'd lost when the building tilted. He pressed his boots hard into the floor, it felt as though he were trying to climb a slick mountain.

The fire had overtaken most of the main living area and was closing on them fast. Without a second glance, Eddie struggled to the ladder and clumsily crouched, then located the first rung with his boot. It was harder to manage with the boy clenched to his front, but there was no time to change positions.

"Hold on tight," Eddie ordered. "We're getting out of here!"

The child nodded against his chest, his face pushing into him hard. Eddie climbed down the leaning ladder. The fire had crawled under the house and was eating at two of the four stilts. Overhead, the wooden floor throbbed.

A loud *crack* shook the structure, and the house dropped two feet. The boy's body tensed against Eddie's torso as his gaze flew to the righthand stilt, which had splintered and was barely holding.

The house groaned, fire spreading over the floor above them.

Making an impromptu decision, Eddie leapt backwards, wrapping his arms around the child as they plummeted down.

Eddie landed with a crouch, still holding the child. In an instant, he hunched over and started running, the crackling fire at his back.

A tumultuous *crash* echoed behind them. The house was leaning aggressively forward and it started to fall, so Eddie kicked it into high gear and barreled away faster than he had ever run before. The heat from the fire seared his back, and smoke and fire shot from the building as it crashed to the ground behind him. He'd barely made it out! He kept running as trees toppled toward him in the wake of the collapse of the burning house.

The rush of heat made Eddie's skin feel like it was melting, but he kept his head tucked and pressed the boy against him as he sped back the way he'd come. *Only a little farther,* he said to himself, unable to say anything aloud. He wasn't out of breath from running, but rather from the smoke he'd been inhaling since this started.

Fire had taken over most of the jungle, and it was

closing in on them. Eddie leapt over a burning log since he couldn't see a clear path around it, then ducked under a curtain of vines and leaves, smoking and singed at the ends. Soon the entire area would be engulfed.

Carrying the boy jostled Eddie's body oddly, but his weight didn't slow him down. The threat of burning to death was motivation enough for him to hurtle through the flames.

Finally, Eddie burst into a clearing where the ground was already charred and the tree stumps were smoking but not afire. This was where it had all started. He halted, and after heaving in a giant breath he tried to unclasp the boy's hands from behind his neck. For a little guy he was strong, and clearly not willing to let go.

"Hey, buddy. You're okay. You're safe," said Eddie, patting the kid on the back gently. The child relaxed a little and slowly pulled away, staring at him with large brown eyes. He cried softly, tears glistening on his cheeks.

"That's it. Take a breath. It's okay," said Eddie.

"Dracott!" a woman yelled in the distance. She ran in their direction with her brown hair flying behind her.

The boy whipped his head around, and another sob emerged from his mouth. He pushed away from Eddie eagerly, dropping to his feet and sprinting for the woman. *"Mommy!"*

When the two met on the charred ground, the woman grabbed her son. She was shaking and crying as she clutched the boy, pinning him into her chest.

Eddie strode toward them, seeking refuge from the heat of the fire at his back. In the distance he saw the team, who were still trying to quell the stubborn fire which had destroyed many homes and much animal habitat in the area.

When Eddie approached the boy and his mother, Dracott's arms were wrapped around his mother's neck and his head was resting on her shoulder like he was ready for a nap after the whole ordeal. The woman rubbed her son's lean back, tears still puddling in her eyes.

"Thank you, sir. I cannot thank you enough for what you did," she said, her voice vibrating with relief.

Eddie smiled at the mother and son, finally reunited.

Julianna approached with a sly grin on her face. She didn't seem relieved to see him safe.

"You're absolutely welcome," said Eddie to the woman. "Now, you two should get as far from the fire as possible. Dracott inhaled a lot of smoke."

The woman nodded and carried her son away.

"You weren't worried about me, were you?" Eddie asked Julianna when she paused beside him to stare at the retreating family.

"When did I have time to worry? I was timing you," she joked.

A laugh popped from his mouth. "What was my time?"

"Two minutes and ten seconds," answered Julianna.

"And you didn't worry even a little bit?"

Julianna cut her eyes at him. "Maybe toward the end, but I knew you were going to get that boy to safety one way or another."

"Poor kid! He was terrified."

"Yeah, fires like this bring chaos. It was a shame that he got lost, but at least you jumped in to save him," said Julianna.

Eddie surveyed the burning jungle. "What do you think? Is there more we can do here?"

"The fire crew said they could use an extra few hands on the eastern perimeter. They're trying to fence in the fires there," said Julianna.

Eddie rubbed his hands together eagerly. They'd had Pip monitor the radios for disasters on nearby planets so Eddie could swoop in and do something brave to break in his newly-enhanced body.

"I'm ready! Let's do this," said Eddie, ambling forward.

"You think you're going to get this *adventuring* thing out of your system soon?" asked Julianna from beside him.

"Does it ever wear off—having these enhancements?"

"No, not really. Not for me, anyway," said Julianna.

Eddie grinned. "Then no. What's the point in having this body and not using it?"

2

Felix Castile's Office, *Unsurpassed*, Tangki System

The red light from the screen on the wall cast an eerie glow in the office. Felix narrowed his eyes, his lips pushing out in a slight grimace. He'd been staring at the image on the screen for a full minute, and it still didn't make sense. That was a rarity for him.

He swiveled to face the scientist sitting on the other side of the desk. "Explain exactly what I'm looking at."

A snotty laugh sputtered from the man's mouth. Elemius was neither tall nor short nor fat nor thin. He was also neither attractive nor ugly. He just *was*, with his plain brown hair and eyes to match. His chuckle fell away once he caught the look of disgust on Felix's face.

"It's really quite simple. I'd assumed you were well versed on chemical compositions," said Elemius, gliding his hand over the top of his head nervously.

Felix sharpened his eyes at the scientist. Elemius was the best. He'd been hard to retain, and he must have known how critical his involvement was or he wouldn't have been so bold.

"I'm well aware what I'm looking at, but I don't understand exactly what it's supposed to be," said Felix, enunciating each word, his hostility palpable.

"Right, well, chemistry isn't for everyone. The same is true of genetic engineering." Elemius cleared his throat as he stood. He pointed at a strand of DNA on the screen. "This example shows a specimen with a nanotechnology-enhanced system."

"I can clearly see that," said Felix, his voice sharp.

"Right, of course you can," said Elemius in a patronizing fashion. "This specimen has additionally been inoculated with a toxin that degenerates the subject's cells on a continuous basis. I call it 'degen' for short."

"That's the reason for the change in the appearance of the DNA sample?" asked Felix. Now this was starting to make sense. He had guessed something was off, but couldn't pinpoint it.

"Precisely," stated Elemius. "Degen overwhelms a center in the body, continuously breaking down the cell membranes and attracting the attention of the nanocytes. As they speed in to fix this area, they reprioritize and focus on repairing the microdamage the toxin is inflicting. This, in turn, stops the nanocytes from enhancing existing cells. That means the subject is unable to heal quickly, fight certain diseases, or revitalize the body. They begin to age naturally as well. So long as the nanocytes are occupied, they are incapable of performing their original tasks."

"You've distracted them, in essence," said Felix.

"Correct," said Elemius. "Which means, if a subject is attacked then they are unable to recover."

"They become purely human again, then?" asked Felix.

"Yes. Once degen is administered, the subject is fully human. They will have zero enhanced abilities. No increased speed, strength, or healing abilities. Degen degrades a person with nanocyte technology back to their original self."

"What if they are put back through the process? Enhanced again using a Pod-doc?" asked Felix, unwilling to celebrate this near-success yet.

Elemius held up a single finger, a triumphant look on his face. "It wouldn't work. Degen will again attract the nanocytes, rendering them useless. Its draw is too strong, and once it has the nanocytes, then it holds them hostage."

"So, there is no way to reverse degen?" asked Felix.

Elemius shrugged. "I'm guessing there could be a way. Destroy the toxin in the system maybe, but it would be incredibly difficult."

Felix allowed a small smile that spoke of his satisfaction. This was it. Finally, he'd figured out a way to destroy General Reynolds. The man was incredibly well- guarded, which posed its own risks. However, even if Felix could get a hit on him, then he'd most likely recover without incident. Felix didn't just want the general to fall, he wanted him to suffer. He wanted him to die like a normal human, vulnerable and defenseless.

Felix felt the urge to laugh. In his mind, he could see the general being inoculated with degen. His eyes would be full of fear as he stared at the barrel of Felix's gun. He'd know how fragile his body was. He'd know that he'd been beaten. He wasn't as strong as he thought. And more than anything, and most important to Felix, was that Lance Reynolds would regret what he'd done. He'd regret turning his back on Felix all those years ago.

When that regret surfaced in General Reynolds' eyes, Felix would pull the trigger.

3

Officers' Lounge, QBS *ArchAngel*, Behemoth System

"You have a strange look on your face," said Eddie. He sat on the other side of a small table from Julianna. It wasn't weird that she'd asked him to meet her at the lounge. It wasn't even strange that she'd indulged him for the last few days, traveling all over the Behemoth System in search of rescue missions. What was strange was the look she was giving him. It was one full of secrets.

"Don't talk about my face," Julianna quipped, trying to act casual. "It's stuck like this. Years and years of dealing with assholes."

Eddie dropped his eyes to the empty shot glass on the table in front of him. He was overdue for a drink. Since he had awakened in the Pod-doc he'd been so consumed with testing his new skills and body that he hadn't had time to relax properly. His body didn't appear much different, although he was firmer and leaner than before. He'd always been in good shape, but now his six-pack was more pronounced. Best of all, he could eat and drink whatever he liked and it didn't matter. He always woke up feeling great, and at the same weight as the day before.

"I happen to like your face, so that's not what I'm talking about. You look like something is irking you. Do you have anything to tell me?" asked Eddie.

Julianna unscrewed the top of the Bacardi 151 and filled both their glasses halfway. "I do, but it's better if I show you," she said, and picked up another bottle—this one ouzo. She poured it into the glasses until they were filled to the brim.

"Wow! Either it's really bad news, or you're trying to get me to take off my pants." Eddie leaned forward and whispered conspiratorially, "Are you wondering if *every-thing* was enhanced?" He winked in an exaggerated manner at her, which earned him a look of mild disgust.

"I'm sure you've been enhanced all over, and you finally feel like a real man," she said with a laugh.

Julianna scooted one of the glasses in Eddie's direction.

"You want me to drink that?" asked Eddie, staring at what he'd describe as a "headache-maker."

"I do." Julianna picked up her own drink, her hand steady, not spilling a drop.

"After I take a sip, are you going to tell me why you look so serious?" asked Eddie.

Julianna shook her head.

"You're *not* going to tell me?" asked Eddie, wondering what could be bothering the Commander.

"No," she answered. "And hey, you're not taking a single sip. I want you to throw back the *whole thing*."

Eddie eyed the full glass. "All right, whatever you say, boss."

"Oh, and it's called a 'Greek Pirate,' by the way." Julianna threw her head back, slamming the shot at once. She rose up, no bitterness on her face from the strong liquor.

"I can only wonder about that drink's name," said Eddie before taking the shot. He had expected it to burn his throat or engulf his insides in fire, but strangely it didn't. He'd also expected the alcohol to have an immediate effect, making him instantly relaxed. That didn't happen either. Then, everything he knew about Julianna's enhancements rushed to the front of his mind. Well, one critical fact, really.

"Teach, you should know that you can't get drunk anymore," said Julianna, echoing what was in his head.

He slammed the glass down with a bit more force than he'd intended. Crew members playing pool and darts nearby looked at them, but quickly covered their interests, giving the captain privacy from their spying eyes.

"Damn it," he said, his voice clear and unchanged by the drink. "Of all the things to take from me, why did it have to be *that*?"

Julianna laughed. "You're alive. Would you rather I'd left you to die?"

The memory of the fire returned to Eddie's mind. He'd been thrown away from the explosion. Commander Lytes had been blown to bits, but Eddie had been far enough away that his body was in one piece. However, enough damage had been inflicted that he should have died.

He picked up the bottle of Bacardi 151 and poured

more into both glasses. "I'll always be grateful that you saved me. And this just means that you and I are very expensive dates now."

Julianna looked at her glass, her eyes still uncertain. Eddie thought there was something she was still holding back, something that seemed to take over her thoughts lately.

"It was the Federation that saved you," she finally said, her tone clipped.

Eddie filled the glasses with the ouzo, a curious look on his face. "So that was it, was it? You were just reluctant to tell me that I can't get drunk? There's nothing else?"

Julianna shook her head, and grabbed the drink as soon as he was done pouring. She threw it back and wiped the back of her hand across her mouth. "Of course, that was it. What else would there be?"

Eddie shrugged before slamming his own drink in one swallow. "Just sense there's something else on your mind."

Julianna's eyes rose to look at the clock on the far wall. Eddie knew that even though it was a fair distance away through the smoky lounge, that she could still easily make out the time. Another benefit of the nanocytes was enhanced sight. It was like having binocular vision.

"We'd better head over to Jack's office. Our meeting starts in a few minutes." Julianna stood, her gaze on the door.

"I guess the boss won't be mad at us for drinking before the meeting, since we can't get drunk anymore," said Eddie with a laugh. "Pros and cons, I suppose."

"Yeah," muttered Julianna. "Pros and cons."

Jack Renfro's Office, QBS *ArchAngel,* Behemoth System

"I'm not sure I asked for your input," Jack was saying to the empty office when Julianna and Eddie entered.

They paused and regarded each other with a bit of confusion, then looked at Jack.

"I believe you said, 'Why can't I ever find anything in this place?'" ArchAngel said from the speaker overhead in an amused tone.

Jack's desk was covered in paper and folders as usual. He used a tablet often, but also seemed partial to paper at times. Julianna kind of found it endearing. He was an incredibly strategic thinker, evolved in his problem-solving approaches, and yet he liked holding a paper report in his hands.

He shook his head at the AI, rolling his eyes for Julianna and Eddie to see. "It was an expression of frustration. It didn't mean that I wanted you to provide a solution."

"But my job is to make *your* job easier. I'm always looking for solutions," said ArchAngel. She was playing with him, trying to get under his skin, and judging by the look on his face it was working.

"I was in my office alone, working. Is there no privacy here?" Jack sounded like he was playing ArchAngel's game, since there was amusement in his tone.

"There's no privacy anywhere on this ship," said the AI, "which is why I'll tell you that the captain and the commander were drinking prior to this scheduled meeting."

Eddie turned to Julianna, shaking his head. "Isn't she a doll?"

"Simply delightful," she said, almost laughing.

Jack sorted through a stack of papers on his desk, craning his neck to look under them. "I think my office *could* use some organization," he admitted.

"I told you so," said ArchAngel.

Jack shook his head. "I knew you were going to say that."

Julianna finally laughed. "It's like you two are married."

"Maybe you should get out more often, Jack," Eddie said.

Jack looked up from the papers and sighed. "I think you're right. Something is wrong with me if my most intimate relationship is with a two-hundred-year-old AI."

No talking for you, Julianna said in her head, preemptively cutting Pip off.

What? I wasn't going to say anything, he lied.

Well, there's *a first.*

I mean, I might have said that you could relate. And as far as getting action goes, I'm about the closest thing to your boyfriend.

A shiver ran over Julianna. *Do not, I repeat, do not* ever *describe yourself as my boyfriend.*

I noted that shiver. I don't know why you have to be so rude. I'd be real good to you, Jules. I'd whisper sweet nothings in your ear.

Julianna gritted her teeth, but kept smiling still. Pip had gotten more playful like this since evolving. It was kind of cute, but she liked pretending that she hated it.

I'm seriously considering having you removed from my head.

Oh! I have a better idea. Why don't you have me

paired with the captain as well? That way I can share a space in both of your heads. I could help you, if you know what I mean. Wink, wink.

There was silence while Julianna cringed.

You do know what I mean? I'm winking right now, said Pip with a laugh.

I don't know what you mean. And having you bouncing back and forth between the two of us might make me crazy.

You'll warm to the idea. It's a good one. Think of all the fun we could have.

I'm thinking about it, and nothing fun is coming to mind. Just endless annoyance.

Sure, sure, Pip said with a hint of mischief in his voice. **Oh, and you don't have to worry about me crossing the platonic boundary. You're not my type.**

A moment later he added, **At all.**

Do you have a crush on ArchAngel, is that it?

Pip made an audible shiver noise of disgust. **Are you kidding me? That woman would have me by the balls. I wouldn't be able to glance at another AI without asking permission.**

Wow, now you have balls. Things have come so far.

It's figurative language, dear Julianna.

Jack was still ruffling through papers and looking overwhelmed. Eddie was peacefully whistling to himself and leaning back in a chair. Julianna took the seat next to him, hoping that Pip was willing to grant her some peace away from his distractions. He was much more fun than he used to be, but hell if she was going to tell him that.

Balls, Pip chirped as Jack cleared his throat.

Julianna suppressed a laugh.

"Here we go. I knew it was in here somewhere," Jack said. He scanned the paper before looking up. "As you are aware—because I keep reminding you of it, —you're overdue to elect an XO. The command structure for Ghost Squadron is unique, since we wanted you two to be equal partners. Because of that, it's growing even more crucial that you have a second in command of this ship."

"What about ArchAngel?" asked Eddie. "She likes to manage everyone."

"Although she takes care of this ship, she wouldn't be right as XO," Jack began. "You see, we as officers *manage* processes, which ArchAngel is superb at. However, she's not really part of your team. This ship is on loan to you, but at some point you will need your own, which means having an XO who can go with you. Archangel will not be able to do that. Her place is here."

"That makes sense," stated Eddie.

Jack laid the report on his desk before tapping it with the tip of his finger. "I'm actually thinking we can kill two birds with one stone here."

The screen behind Jack's head flickered and revealed an image of a rotating planet.

"Wow, you and ArchAngel have really coordinated your act," said Eddie.

Jack didn't look impressed. He shook his head and said dully, "Yes, sometimes it feels like she's listening to my thoughts."

"What planet is that?" asked Julianna, trying to keep the meeting on track.

"Right," said Jack, wheeling around to look at the

screen. "This is Klamath. It's a small planet, largely covered in ice."

Julianna noticed that much of the planet was entirely white. There were bodies of water and masses of greenish land, but not many.

"You want us to go to an ice planet? I'm glad you reserved this until after I was upgraded," said Eddie with a laugh. He leaned over and whispered loudly to Julianna. "We have resistance to cold, right?"

She nodded, keeping her gaze forward.

"Aside from requesting that you elect an XO, I've also been thinking that Ghost Squadron needs a Special Forces unit. What you all did on Nexus was impressive considering you didn't have ground forces. However, I don't want you to go into a similar situation in the future without having your own detachment."

"I'm not sure I'm following you," said Julianna, continuing to stare at the rotating planet of Klamath.

Jack nodded like he understood her confusion. "There's a squad of Special Forces soldiers stationed on Klamath. They were set up by the Federation under General Reynolds, about like Ghost Squadron. Specifically, they are located in the northern hemisphere on a small bit of unnamed land. The natives are considered savages, and this team was sent there to quell the warfare."

"You want us to retrieve this Special Forces team? Recruit them?" asked Eddie.

"Wouldn't we be pulling them away from their mission?" asked Julianna.

Jack shrugged reluctantly. "Unfortunately, although this team is considered quite skilled, they haven't been able to prevent the attacks. Sometimes we can go in and create peace. Sometimes we can't."

"So, the forces are being pulled out?" asked Julianna.

"Exactly. And this team is being reassigned to Ghost Squadron, which I suspect they will enjoy much more than their current assignment," said Jack.

"Yeah, not having frostbitten balls would be a welcome change for most," said Eddie.

Balls, Pip said in Julianna's head before returning to being quiet like before.

She rolled her eyes.

"We've tried to relay the change in orders to Lieutenant Chad Fletcher," said Jack. "However, the natives have them practically overrun. Any communications in or out of the planet have been compromised."

"So, you need us to buzz over there, help them out, and tell them to report to their new base of operations, is that right?" asked Eddie.

"Correct," stated Jack. He then lowered his gaze, his eyes suddenly heavy. "Surveillance shows that the Special Ops team is still strong in numbers, however, like I said, they're close to being overwhelmed."

"So, you're sending us into a war," said Julianna. She had read the change in Jack's tone and the tension in his shoulders.

"The natives are unreasonable, and our attempts to intervene appear to only have pissed them off further," said Jack.

"These natives? Are you going to give us a hint as to why you refer to them as savage, or is it a surprise?" asked Eddie.

"I'll have Officer Sours brief you on that. She's studied the Mamaths, as they are called," said Jack.

"Mamaths?" asked Eddie. "They sound quaint."

"As quaint as a giant bunny rabbit with razor-sharp teeth," said Jack.

Julianna let out a long breath. This was a dangerous mission to undertake right after Eddie's upgrade. He was still getting used to his body, and that would take time. "This Special Ops team you want us to pick up—are you sure they are worth us going out to this planet?"

"I could send a carrier ship." Jack mused for a moment, and then shook his head, deciding against the idea. "No, I think it should be you folks who bring in the team. They are under serious fire, and getting out of there will be an ordeal. Furthermore, I want you to see the team in action, and vice versa. First impressions are everything. Adding a Special Forces unit to Ghost Squadron isn't something I take lightly."

"We will need both Q-Ships, is that right?" asked Eddie.

"Yes, and take a few Black Eagles for cover as well. You'll understand more once you speak with Marilla," said Jack.

"You mentioned killing two birds with one stone," said Julianna. "Something about this and the XO?"

"Right, I did," said Jack. "Lieutenant Fletcher has been leading this team of twelve for several years. He's well respected by his team, makes sound decisions, and is an incredibly skilled soldier. I also think that he is the natural choice for your XO. However, you're going to have to bring him in first. Get to know the guy. Have him on the ship."

Eddie slapped his hands together and looked at Julianna. "You ready to grow the family?"

She nodded reluctantly. This was the correct thing to do. It felt right to grow Ghost Squadron, but still she knew she'd always value the time when the team had been small. She'd always think fondly of its inception.

Intelligence Center, QBS *ArchAngel*, Behemoth System

Eddie chuckled at the image of a gorilla-looking creature covered in long white fur on the largest screen over Chester's workstation. Long black claws protruded from its giant fingers, and its beady eyes were tiny on its massive head.

"That's one ugly caveman," said Eddie, still laughing at the cartoonish-looking creature.

"That," said Chester, pointing at the screen, "is one of the angry natives you will have to fight on Klamath."

Eddie's laughter ended abruptly. He turned to Marilla, looking for confirmation. "What? Is that true?"

She nodded, pushing her hair behind her ear. "Yes, this species is known as the Mamath. They used to be widespread on Klamath, but due to their violent nature they have killed each other to the point of near extinction."

"Why has the Federation been silently interfering?" asked Julianna.

"One of the reasons was to help preserve the Mamath population," explained Marilla. "At least that's how I understand it from reviewing the reports, but I think that mission has been abandoned. Also, the Mamaths weren't only killing off their own population, but also the other animals on the planet. Putting the Special Ops team down there was an attempt to make peace for all. However, I don't think there's any hope for the Mamath. They've been trying not to use deadly force on this species, but it's not working."

"Which just means they've been getting their asses handed to them, right?" asked Eddie.

Marilla nodded in confirmation. "That's how I understand it, but my clearance on this is low."

"So, the Mamaths are angry brute-types. Anything else you can add?" asked Eddie.

"They aren't very intelligent. The frontal lobe of this alien species is incredibly underdeveloped, which is the cause of their volatile nature," said Marilla.

Julianna spun to face Eddie with a serious look on her face. "Maybe you're half Mamath."

"Ha-ha, Jules. We all know that I'm as cuddly as a teddy bear. I just choose to kick ass to keep things spinning round and round," said Eddie.

"Teddy bear, huh?" asked Chester measuring Eddie up. "I never took you as the teddy bear type, but it's a cute description."

Eddie pointed at the hacker and smiled. "You're the cute one, Chester. And you owe me a game of pool in the lounge when I get back."

"Got it, Captain," said Chester with a salute.

"Marilla, what else can you tell us about the Mamaths? Anything that Lieutenant Fletcher's team might not know that we can use to help the cause?" asked Julianna.

"Actually, there is something that I knew about the alien species, but the team didn't know when they were deployed," Marilla stated.

"What's that?" asked Eddie, immediately intrigued.

"They don't like fire," said Hatch from the doorway.

After Hatch interrupted the meeting with perfect timing, Eddie and Julianna followed him back to his workstation next to the cargo bay. Apparently, Marilla had fed the mechanic/scientist the information, and he'd been able to pull some technology from his locker.

"I guess I shouldn't be shocked that these snow monsters are frightened by fire," said Eddie when they paused in the lab.

"I'd be surprised if anything logical occurred to you," said Hatch, waddling over to Knox, who was holding a weapon of sorts. It had a long hose like a fire extinguisher with an insulated nozzle on the end, which attached to a tank with straps on it.

"Go ahead and set up the targets," Hatch ordered Knox. He nodded and ran off to the other side of the room.

Knox had been working with Hatch since he'd been injured. Now, he was better and in more ways than just physically. Julianna had spied him smiling a time or two, which had caught her off-guard the first time. The grin transformed his face, making his oft-troubled eyes appear young, matching his features. Before that he'd previously looked like a kid who had been asked to shoulder too much responsibility too young. But here, Knox nearly had a skip in his walk.

Knox pushed three metal statues from the back of the area, up to the front, only a few yards away.

"I've created a flame thrower, in essence," said Hatch, indicating the hose and the tank it was attached to.

Eddie rubbed his hands together. "Oh, now you're talking, Doc!"

Hatch ignored the captain and glanced at Julianna. "From what I can tell, reading Marilla's report, bullets and other weapons are mostly ineffective against Mamaths. They have thick fur and a hide that's really hard to pierce. Your best bet is fire."

"But we don't want to kill them," Julianna stated.

"No, they are dying out," said Hatch, waving one of his tentacles in the air at her. "I read the report, so I know. But you want to survive and not be killed either. Fire will burn these monsters, and it will also scare the hell out of them. Just depends on how you play things. Strategy is *your* game. Mine is weapons."

"Which is why we make a great team," stated Eddie, eyeing the fire blaster contraption.

"The tank straps on your back. I have exactly three fire blasters, so you should be set," stated Hatch, right as Lars entered the work area.

Eddie waved the Kezzin over. He'd been ordered to report to them once it was clear they'd need extra forces on the mission. He'd be fully briefed in later. Lars was a quick study. He could join a mission halfway through orientation and do fine.

"As I was saying," Hatch continued, "All you have to do is strap on the tank, hold the hose in the direction of the target, and fire." One of Hatch's tentacles pointed the nozzle at the first statue, which was roughly fifteen feet away. Another tentacle pulled a lever on the bottom of the tank, which would be easy to access when it was strapped to ones back.

Fire shot from the end of the hose and across the space. It enveloped the statue of a nondescript man, covering it in seconds. Hatch released the lever and the fire disappeared at once. Before anyone could say a word, he pivoted the nozzle an inch to the right and pulled the trigger again, taking out the second statue stationed a few feet over and back from the first. Then not turning the lever to off, he swerved the hose to the third statue. Fire trailed between the two statues until the last one was engulfed. Hatch released the lever and turned matter-of-factly to the group.

"Any questions?" he asked, looking to be suppressing a proud smile.

"Aim and shoot. I think I got this," said Eddie, walking over and eagerly taking the fire blaster from Hatch.

"Just remember… You can cook your dinner with this fire or you can cook yourself," warned Hatch.

"The only thing I plan on roasting is the enemy," said Eddie, giving him a sly wink.

5

Alpha-line Q-Ship, Planet Klamath, Behemoth System

"I don't understand why you always get to fly the good ship," Eddie said over the comm, pretending to sound bitter.

"Because I'm older," stated Julianna, focusing on the snow-covered terrain below them. "Besides, Hatch says he's close to having another Alpha-line Q-Ship ready for us."

"Then this bad boy will be yours, Carnivore," said Eddie to Lars over the comm.

Lars had made incredible progress on the Q-Ship simulators. He wasn't just an excellent pilot, but was also proving to be a solid decisionmaker when in battle. That wasn't always easy when enemy fire was coming at you.

"Pip has identified the area behind those caves on the eastern side to be the best place to land," explained Julianna.

"Why is he not talking to me? I thought he could interface through the ships," Eddie asked.

Should I tell him that you don't want to share me? asked Pip in Julianna's head.

I never said that, she grumbled.

No, but you're thinking it.

I'm not either. I'm only trying to keep things organized, and having you in the captain's head simply doesn't make sense.

Are you sure you're not afraid it would erase the walls? You've spent many decades building those iron clad walls. What if we break them down? What if we—

Have you deleted, said Julianna, cutting Pip off.

I can't be so easily deleted.

Can't you? Let's find out.

Julianna landed the cloaked ship on a cushion of snow. Everything on Klamath was covered in a soft blanket of ice. It was kind of beautiful, if one could forget that eight-foot monsters owned the planet and liked to tear the heads off anything they came across.

Julianna zipped up the thermal jacket she'd been given by Hatch. It had almost made her sweat inside the Q-Ship, but she suspected it wouldn't feel so hot when she stepped onto Klamath's arctic terrain.

She had Pip lower the hatch and spied Lars and Eddie walking out of the hatch of their own ship. Julianna knelt over and pulled the flamethrower from the floor. She strapped it on and reinforced it into place, holding the nozzle with her right hand.

"Ready to burn shit up?" Eddie asked when she joined them. Each of their footsteps had left prints behind marking their trek from the cloaked Q-Ships. It was fine though, since they had a short jaunt between the landing area and where the Special Forces were rumored to be stationed.

"Almost," she said, holding up a hand to Eddie. Lars stood beside him, surveying the whiteness around them, his eyes intense.

Pip, inform the Black Eagles of our location. We're heading in and will need coverage from the sky, Julianna said in her head.

I'm already on it. Black Eagles in place and ready for your command, stated Pip.

Thanks. We're headed into the mouth of the beast.

As always, be careful.

Julianna nodded, taking a steadying breath. Each mission was different, with its own unique challenges. One might think that after two hundred years it got easier, but that wasn't how battle worked. Each day was unique, and so was each fight. It's the soldier who took this uniqueness for granted who was most in danger. Complacency was the greatest weakness.

"All right, let's go," said Julianna, taking the lead position. "Look alive."

Julianna marched through the snow a few paces ahead of Eddie and Lars. Their boots crunched loudly, and the sound echoed off the hills ahead of them. In the distance there was a stand of trees. Marilla had explained that these were known as shelter belts. They appeared all over this land, and created barriers for the habitable areas.

Pointing to the shelter belt, Julianna made eye contact

with Eddie. He nodded in agreement before she ambled forward.

The air was thick with moisture, and it was so cold that it burned Eddie's cheeks and nose. There was no breeze, though, and for that he was glad. The sky was a dull gray, but the brightness of the snow and ice made him squint. Their jackets and thermal pants matched the snow, making them blend easily into their surroundings.

A rustling sound made all three freeze. Julianna held up a hand, pausing them. They were between two snow hills, with prairie in front of them.

The rustling increased, sounding like a man or an alien or an animal was approaching on the other side of the hill. Julianna turned, aiming the flamethrower in the direction of the noise.

Eddie watched as her shoulders tensed. She was hyper-alert, even more so than usual. Something about this snow planet had her on edge, and he thought it had to do with him. Maybe he was reading too much into it, though.

More noise, but louder than before. Whatever was on the other side of the hill was close. Then something as white as the snow hopped out. It took Eddie a moment to register what he was seeing. The small round bunny-like animal paused. It stared up at the three poised soldiers, its enormous brown eyes wide with curiosity. The creature was larger than most rabbits—about the size of a basketball. Its pointed ears stuck straight up.

"Oh, fuck," whispered Julianna. She relaxed a bit, lowering the nozzle of her flamethrower.

"Don't shoot the poor little bunny," teased Eddie.

Julianna cast a look of agreement over her shoulder.

"That bunny almost got wasted."

One of the bunny's ears twitched and then swiveled to take in a noise. Eddie's enhanced hearing also told him that something else was approaching. Maybe a pack of bunnies? Then they'd be overwhelmed with cuteness.

The bunny's head jerked to the side and it darted the opposite direction, hopping more furiously than when it had appeared.

Julianna looked back at Eddie, her expression tentative. As she was turning back around, a wolf sprang from behind the hill. The animal halted in the spot where the bunny had been and sniffed the snow. Then, noticing the three, he lifted his head and bared his teeth at them, growling deep in his throat. He had thick white and gray fur and was twice the size of Harley, who was a pretty large dog—or at least Eddie had thought so.

Julianna reached for the lever on the bottom of the flamethrower. Her movements were careful to avoid spooking the wolf.

"What are you doing?" hissed Eddie.

"Getting rid of an animal who wants to eat us," said Julianna in a quiet voice.

The wolf took a step forward, growling louder.

"It's just a wolf. Remember what Marilla said…endangered species?" said Eddie.

"Do you have a fucking bone? Because I'm fresh out," said Julianna.

A loud rustling filled the air. The wolf animal turned, looking in the direction it had come. Then a pack of wolves ran out from behind the hill. The new arrivals halted, having caught the sight of the three. The scout hopped at the wolf in the front. It was as if he were saying, "Look what I found."

"Fuck," Julianna whispered. "Can I fire at them or do you want to pet one of these dogs?"

The wolves advanced, making the three shuffle back a few steps. The beasts' intent was clear. They were hungry, and the team would feed them for days.

"No, fuck these mutts. Fire away!" yelled Eddie. He stepped forward, so he was beside Julianna. Lars did the same, so they formed a wall.

Julianna pulled the lever. Fire shot from her weapon, but she had aimed it downward. The effect was immediate. The wolves retreated behind the hill at once, unharmed by the heat that had melted the snow in front of them. She released the lever to cut off the stream.

"So, you *do* have a heart," said Eddie, looking at her with a proud smile.

"I figured I didn't have to roast them. Just get them to retreat," said Julianna. She trudged forward, stomping through the new puddle of water, and after a cursory glance around she let out a sigh of relief. "All clear."

Eddie caught up with her easily. "Wonder what other animals are waiting out there to eat us?"

"Besides Mamaths? Something tells me there are all sorts of fierce creatures on this planet," said Julianna.

"You good?" Eddie asked the Kezzin. He noticed Lars was shivering, even though he was wearing thermal clothing like theirs.

Lars nodded, his pointy teeth ramming together as he violently shivered. "I'm fine. Kezzin aren't really equipped for the cold."

"Will you be all right?" asked Eddie.

"I'll be fine. I just need to get moving," said Lars.

"Agreed," said Eddie. He pointed to the shelter belt. "From the air it looked like there was a camp set up over there."

"Let's hope it's our Special Ops team," said Julianna, taking the lead again and hiking in that direction.

An explosion shook the ground, and a plume of smoke blossomed over the trees. Julianna spun, giving Eddie a cautious look. Lately they mostly communicated with looks rather than words.

He nodded, and they both sprang into action, sprinting across the snow, toward the belt. It became denser halfway through the pasture, almost up to their knees.

"Hey!" yelled Lars from behind them. He aimed his flamethrower at the ground and pulled the lever and the snow instantly melted, making the trek in front of him easier.

"Good idea," said Eddie. He relished the idea of using the flamethrower for the first time. He pulled the lever and fire roared from the nozzle like a stream of water. It melted the snow in front of them, and when he'd taken care of the next twenty feet they took off running as he kept the stream of fire flowing continuously. The path was slushy, but much easier to traverse.

Julianna sprinted the last few yards and then threw her back against a tree. The explosions had continued, and were now joined by gunfire.

"Sounds like we got here at the right time," said Eddie from beside her.

"Or the wrong time, depending on your perspective,"

she agreed.

Three Black Eagles streaked overhead, racing toward the explosions. A moment later Julianna said, "The Mamaths have the squadron surrounded. They are backed up to the shelter belt."

"Okay, then let's spread out," said Eddie. "Lars, you head south, and I'll go north. Jules, you stay here. We'll head through the trees and come out on the other end, with our flamethrowers blazing. We need to get to them before it's too late."

Lars nodded.

Julianna only stared, a tentative look in her eyes. "Be careful. Don't do anything stupid," she said after a short moment.

"I wouldn't dream of it," said Eddie, spinning around and sprinting north, through the trees.

The shelter belt was thick, about fifteen yards of closely-positioned evergreens. Still, Julianna could see blasts from the explosions ahead through the trees.

We're going to try and push the Mamaths back. The Black Eagles need to support our efforts once they are far enough from the camp, she said to Pip.

Copy that. It appears that the Mamaths found this spot just now, surprising the platoon.

Maintain a visual from above and let me know if anything changes.

You mean, watch your back?

Exactly.

Julianna crouched so she could brush through the tree branches more easily. It was warmer in the shelter belt, but not by much. It was also like pushing through an over-stocked closet of prickly clothes.

Soldiers were darting into the trees ahead. They had been pushed back as far as they could go. These guys would be sorely grateful for this surprise visit.

"Hey!" she yelled to a guy three trees in front of her, and he spun around, with a rifle in his hands and fear in his eyes. He squinted at her for several seconds. It took him a moment to register what he was seeing.

"We're with the Federation. Here to help you out," she yelled.

Relief flooded the guy's face. "You aren't a moment too soon."

A loud explosion rocked the ground. Both Julianna and the soldier ducked to protect their faces from the debris that flooded the shelter belt. A second blast sent a heat wave into them. The explosions were probably keeping the Mamaths back, but apparently weren't enough.

"Where's the brunt of the attack coming from?" asked Julianna, scooting up beside the soldier.

He pointed at a clearing she could plainly see from where she was sitting. The Federation troops were hunkered down behind crates and half-destroyed tents. The Mamaths, which were much more menacing in person, thundered through the camp. They tore through tents with flicks of their wrists. The giants were impossibly tall, almost towering over the trees around them.

"Where's your lieutenant?" asked Julianna.

The guy scanned the chaos and pointed to a pair of

soldiers barricaded behind a huge boulder. It was at the edge of the camp, close to the approaching Mamaths.

"The one on the right," he yelled over another explosion.

The lieutenant pulled a pin from a grenade and threw it at the closest Mamath. Then he and the other soldiers ducked and covered their ears. Snow exploded, causing the Mamath to fall and scuttle backward. Julianna expected that to be the end of it, but a few seconds later the undeterred beast pushed itself to its feet.

"Stubborn assholes, aren't they?" mused Julianna.

"You have no idea," the guy said, sounding weary.

"Stay here," said Julianna, rising to a standing position.

"You can't go out there. They'll eat you for lunch," said the guy frantically.

"Don't worry, I'm not on the menu." Julianna sprinted head-down in the direction of Lieutenant Fletcher. He was wearing a puffy white coat like hers and on his head was a white cap, which, now that Julianna thought about it, might have helped poor Lars.

Fletcher turned in time to see Julianna approach and had a similar reaction to the first soldier's. How long had it been since this group had seen outsiders?

"I'm here to help. The Federation sent me," yelled Julianna. She threw her back up against the rock when she met them.

"Who are you?" asked Fletcher, taking deep breaths. A nearby explosion made them all duck. The Mamaths were close. *Too* close.

"I'm with a classified unit like yours, and the general has reassigned you to us. We're taking you out of here," said Julianna, glancing over the rock. There was an approaching Mamath about twenty yards away.

"I saw the orders, but we've been a little busy," said Fletcher. "Command said reinforcements were on the way, but I gotta tell you, lady—I expected more."

"We're all the help you need," she said. "Are you ready for extraction?"

"To where?" he asked. "The mission report didn't say, which is one of the many annoying aspects of working off the books."

"The QBS *ArchAngel*. You're going to assist Ghost Squadron," said Julianna.

Fire, loud and bright, shot from the north, which meant Eddie was on the scene. Several Mamaths ran in the opposite direction to another shelter belt in the distance.

"*ArchAngel*? You've got to be kidding me! Who *are* you?" asked Fletcher.

"Commander Julianna Fregin," she explained, "and I'm totally serious. You want off this cold-ass planet or don't you?"

"Holy Hell!" Fletcher blinked and dropped his jaw, his pale-blue eyes suddenly stunned, then saluted. "Commander Fregin. I had no idea. What an honor this is. I've heard stories about you from the war. You're—"

"Forget that," she snapped. "Focus on the job and let's get you boys out of here."

"Yes, of course," he said with a chuckle. "But it's not every day you get to meet a legend. We're ready to move on your mark, ma'am."

"Your men, are they scattered?" asked Julianna. "How dispersed from this position are they?"

"It looks like they are mostly headed this way," said Fletcher, pointing.

Half a dozen soldiers were racing toward them with the fire at their backs. Eddie was showing off.

She popped up and realized that the Mamath that had been approaching was only ten feet away. He was dumber than the rest, apparently, and bigger, too. At his back were two others and they formed a giant wall, their eyes narrowed and steam pouring from their nostrils.

"Okay, round up your men. We're heading out," said Julianna, standing and facing the Mamaths.

"We'll never get out of here in time. They have us surrounded. And by the time we get through the shelter belt it will be too late," said Fletcher.

"That was an order, Lieutenant," said Julianna. She could see Eddie, in the distance, firing at each approaching Mamath. Some fled when he fired. Some merely held up their arm to shield, being a safe enough distance from the flame.

"Yes, Commander," said Fletcher at her back.

She threw up her chin, looking at the Mamath ahead who had just noticed her. "How you doing, ugly?"

The monster grunted and then opened his mouth and yelled so loud it hurt her ears.

"What?" she asked. "I think you said you're cold, is that right?"

She stood with her feet apart, one hand on the nozzle and the other on the lever.

The Mamath stomped, making the ground vibrate. Then he hunched low and charged in her direction. She pulled on the lever and a steady stream of hot-ass fire spilled from the hose, knocking straight into the Mamath. He caught on fire at once and it spread over his front, shoulders and head. Madly, the monster threw himself into the snow and rolled, trying to extinguish himself.

They might have been stupid, but they knew to stop, drop and roll. *That was something*, Julianna thought.

The Mamaths who had flanked the first had shielded their faces from the fire. They peeked out of their clawed fingers, like scared children.

"Are you cold, too?" Julianna yelled across the snow at them.

She pulled the lever and fire again streamed from the thrower. Behind the bright fire she made out the visual of the Mamaths retreating. The first was on hands and knees, crawling away.

To the south, more soldiers were fleeing in their direction. Lars was there, blasting through the crowd of Mamaths, making them retreat.

Julianna was about to celebrate a near victory when she turned to Eddie. He was blasting away Mamaths, but didn't see that one had back tracked. The beast was behind him, approaching, looking to fucking tip toe across the snow.

"Teach!" yelled Julianna.

He looked up at her, still streaming fire, keeping back two Mamaths that were trying hard to get to him.

She indicated to his back, but the Mamath then lunged at Teach. Julianna sprinted at once, abandoning her position. Eddie turned, but before he could whip the fire in that direction, the Mamath picked him up by the base of his coat and slung him through the air. He collided with the first row of prickly evergreens.

Julianna released her fire at once, yelling loudly at the monster. The fire blasted him straight in the chest, knocking him back. She doubled back, shooting fire the entire time.

Eddie lay at the base of trees, but was pushing up when she approached.

"You alright?" she asked, keeping the Mamaths at bay.

"Yeah, I'll survive." He groaned, disconnecting himself from the branches of a stubborn tree.

Send in the Black Eagles. We're ready to get the fuck out of here, Julianna said to Pip.

You got it boss, he replied.

A moment later, the three Black Eagles soared overhead, from the tree line. Once they'd passed the line where the Special Forces were they began firing, pushing the Mamath back.

"Come on Teach. Let's get out of here," she yelled, as he pulled away from the trees where he'd been lodged. He looked a bit battered from the assault, but mostly fine. She knew something like this was going to happen.

"But I didn't get to make a snow man," he pretended to complain.

"Next time," she said.

Fletcher had rounded up most of his men. Lars ran in their direction, having been relieved by the Black Eagles.

"Through the trees. Our ships are on the other side of the clearing," ordered Julianna.

"You heard the commander," yelled Fletcher, a wide smile on his face. He had probably never been so relieved. "Let's get the hell out of this shithole!"

6

Officers' Lounge, QBS *ArchAngel*, Behemoth System

The lounge on the QBS *ArchAngel* felt extra small with all the new Special Ops team taking up every barstool. Chester stopped in the entryway and almost turned around, but he spied a guy leaning over next to Marilla on the pretext of helping her line up a shot at the pool table. Wasn't that the oldest trick in the book? *Oh, honey, let me show you how to do it, with my body pressed against yours.* Chester didn't laugh at his internal banter as he usually did.

The soldier had a brown flat-top, large biceps, and a barrel chest. He could no doubt bench-press Chester's nerdy self.

Marilla stepped to the side and shook her head, looking nervous. That was a good sign. Her nonverbal cues said she wasn't into him.

Chester ambled over with a bit more swagger than usual.

"Hey Mar, have you seen the captain?" asked Chester. He knew exactly where the captain was. You'd have to be blind and deaf not to see him holding court at the bar, telling a story to half a dozen of the Special Ops team. His arms waved wildly as he described something in his tall tale.

"Chest! Hi!" Marilla squeaked, looking relieved to see him. Was he imagining that? Hoping for the reaction?

"'Chest?'" the meathead repeated.

"Chester," the hacker corrected him. "I'm *the* Chester Wilkerson."

"'The?' Like you're someone important?" asked the flat-top.

Chester sorted through fifteen different insults to determine the perfect one, but before he could use it the jerk-face laughed.

"I've never heard of you." The man laid his arm around Marilla's shoulder and an uncomfortable expression jumped to her face. "Should I know who this guy is?" he asked her.

"You should, but you've been stuck on an ice cube of a planet so I get that you're a bit sheltered," Chester quipped.

Marilla shrugged out from under the guy's arm. He cast her an annoyed look and said, "Someone has to fight the good fight. That was why they brought us here." He looked Chester up and down, taking in his frayed jeans and T-shirt. "I'm guessing you're a civilian, is that right?"

Marilla grabbed Chester's hand and pulled him toward the bar. "Come on, the captain is over here."

He had hardly registered that she'd yanked him away

from the thug because her hand was in his. "Hey, you didn't give me a chance to answer that brute."

Marilla halted and her eyes swiveled up to meet Chester's. "What does it matter?"

Chester glanced down at their still-intertwined hands. "It mattered to me."

Marilla yanked her hand away and put it on her hip. "You could have told him that you're the best hacker in this galaxy and he wouldn't have cared. His type doesn't put stock in intelligence. They think we're safe and free because they fight, but what they don't get is that people like you and me do a lot behind the scenes. Things that really matter."

She was absolutely radiant right then with the passion burning in her brown eyes. Marilla had always been beautiful, but this fire made her come alive in a new way.

"You don't think I'm the best hacker in this galaxy?" asked Chester, feigning offense.

Marilla rolled her eyes, then turned for the bar and said as she stalked off, "Chester Wilkerson, you are absolutely impossible."

"And you can't get enough of me," he sang, strolling with a bit more confidence than before.

"I'm not kidding. He was *this* big," said Eddie, holding his hand over his head.

"Whoa, and you kicked his ass?" Lieutenant Chad Fletcher asked. He, like everyone on his team, had cleaned up and changed into a fresh uniform. Fletcher had a bald head and an easy smile. He appeared to be the same age as most on his team, but there was a maturity in his eyes.

"Oh, hell no. I got my ass handed to me," said Eddie with a loud laugh. "But when the savage thought I had passed out and turned his back, I jumped him and ran his head through the bar."

The crowd around them howled with laughter. Julianna took a long drink, staring around. She'd been quiet most of the evening, allowing Eddie to hold the spotlight. It was better for her if people found her unassuming. That way when she took charge, they took notice.

"I thought you said the commander was there," said Fletcher.

Eddie nodded, beaming at Julianna. "She was there the second time. I was about to have my ass handed to me that time too."

"Because he likes trouble," said Julianna, mostly into her glass.

"It's true. I do. But Jules stepped in and saved the day, just like on Klamath," said Eddie.

"You would have been alright both times," said Julianna.

"Yeah, but it's more fun if we get to tag team in these fights," said Eddie.

Fletcher emptied his beer, thumping it on the bar with a satisfied sigh. "I have to tell you, Commander, when you arrived on Klamath and said you were pulling us out of there, I thought an angel had just fallen."

The men and women around him cheered. They all wore wide smiles. Each was grateful to be aboard the QBS *ArchAngel* and not fighting Mamaths.

Julianna laughed. How could she not? In all her life, no one had described her as an angel.

"Yeah, I bet you're actually too warm on this ship after being on that cold-ass planet," said Eddie.

Fletcher blew out a breath as he shook his head. "You have no idea. And not only is the environment better, but it sounds like you people have fun."

"We try to keep it entertaining," said Eddie. "What's the point in kicking dickwads around and not having a giggle while you do it?"

The crowd around Eddie erupted in laughter, and he lapped up the attention.

"Hey, Captain," called Chester. His normally pale face was a bit flushed. "We still on for that game of pool?"

Eddie looked at the hacker and his mouth broke into a smile. "You know it! I hear you're a pool shark, and want to see this firsthand." Fletcher and many of the others slapped Eddie on the back as he passed them. He nodded to the crowd as he left. As soon as he was gone, the space fell uncomfortably quiet. It almost felt darker, like he had carried a light with him.

Julianna dismissed herself and strode for the exit. Once in the corridor, she welcomed the silence. Sitting by the wall as if waiting for someone was their scruffy dog Harley. Reflexively Julianna flinched, remembering the wolves, but the playful look in Harley's eyes was completely different from the menacing anger on the wolves' faces.

"What, are dogs not allowed in the lounge?" Julianna asked dryly.

Harley yipped back excitedly.

"Maybe I should go back in there then," she teased, walking down the hallway. Harley followed her, looking down at the deck and then back up at her expectantly.

Julianna halted and glanced down at the dog. He sat and stared up at her, his mouth wide open and tongue spilling over the side. "Tell me, what exactly are you so happy about?"

Harley, as if on cue, mumbled a bit in his dog voice.

"That made zero sense," complained Julianna.

He barked loudly in reply.

"Seriously, I don't get you at all. You're happy all the time. You do nothing but play and sleep, and you're liked by most everyone," said Julianna.

Harley lifted one of his paws as if offering her a handshake.

"And yes, I said *most* everyone. Assume away." She turned and walked off, and the smelly and shedding fleabag followed dutifully beside her.

General Reynolds' Office, QBS _ArchAngel_, Behemoth System

"Well, well, well. Here's our favorite general and mystery man," said Eddie upon entering Lance's office. The general had asked ArchAngel to send word to Julianna and Eddie that he was aboard.

Julianna saluted, her back straight.

Lance smiled modestly and indicated the two chairs beside Jack. "Please join us."

"You didn't tell us we were getting a surprise visit from the general," Eddie said to Jack.

"That was because, as you mentioned, it was a _surprise_," said Jack.

"Touché." Eddie winked.

"I informed Jack that as soon as I had a chance then I'd be stopping by," said Lance. "That was once he'd told me that the man behind these attacks on the fringe was Felix Castile. I asked him to keep the information in confidence, and told him I'd brief you two in person at my earliest convenience."

"Oh, good—you're going to shed a bit of light on that power-hungry spit-fuck," said Eddie.

Lance picked up his unlit cigar and rolled it in his fingers. "I don't think what I have to share will shine too much light on the man. It's hard to understand why some take such a vindictive path when peace is clearly the better option, but they keep us in business, and I suspect they always will."

"Peace isn't an option to those who are consumed by greed, sir," said Julianna.

Lance nodded appreciatively. "Well put, Commander." He set the cigar back down on the desk and regarded the three in front of him for a moment before saying, "Felix Castile, as you already know, is a powerful, intelligent, and wealthy man. He's self-made, which normally I'd respect the hell out of. Nevertheless, for all of his positive attributes, he's still a fucking asshole. Give a man brains, wealth and prestige and it won't matter if, at his core, he's rotten.

"The Federation had employed Felix in different roles. We were planning the first major transport mission back to Earth," explained Lance. "Felix had insisted that his loyalty to the Federation and service meant he'd have a place on that transport ship. He believed he had earned the right to go, largely because of his wealth and connections, but that's not how it works."

Lance fell silent suddenly, chewing on the inside of his cheek.

"Felix was rejected?" asked Jack, finally.

Lance nodded. "He was furious. He said I denied him

the chance to finally go home, back to where he believed he belonged. Where humanity belonged. He felt betrayed, like I had taken his birthright. I've thought about this throughout the years, and I stand by my decision. It doesn't matter who you are or what you've done. That mission was critical, and Felix didn't need to be on that ship. He *wanted* to be, but I get requests every day from people who want something. I can't grant them all. Most accept this and move on, but I knew from the beginning that Felix wasn't likely to let it go. He became more volatile than ever. I suspected he was planning something to get back at me for my decision." Lance sighed and shook his head. "I received a report that he was planning an attack, so I sent forces after him. There was an explosion, and several casualties. I concluded that he was dead, but now I know the truth."

"Felix faked his own death?" asked Julianna.

"I suspect so," Lance confirmed. "He has been on the fringe ever since, plotting and planning this all. I see it now. And whatever he is up to, it's been a long time coming. I have a feeling he's preparing to strike hard, so we need to be ready when he does."

"Fortunately, we've just added a Special Ops team to the crew," Jack stated.

Lance nodded approvingly. "That's a good start. What you've done so far has secured our footing in this silent war. More than anything, we have to find out what Felix is planning. He's damn brilliant and will certainly be hatching something that he hopes will knock our feet out from under us."

"That's not going to happen," Eddie said with conviction.

"That's the spirit, Captain," said Lance. "Have your intelligence team dig for more information. Your new soldiers will come in handy when it's time to fight, but don't forget to use all your assets."

"Chester and Marilla are the best. They'll work around the clock," declared Eddie.

"Good. In the meantime, I have a mission for you and the new Special Ops team," said Lance.

Eddie's pulse quickened. "Oh boy! Whose ass are we going after?"

"No ass-kicking yet," said Lance, "but not to worry, there will be plenty of that soon."

Eddie smiled easily. "Yeah, I figured as much."

"I think," began Lance, "that we should break in the new team with a humanitarian mission. Something that shows them what Ghost Squadron is all about. It protects freedoms when necessary, but more importantly, it restores hope."

The screen behind Lance changed to an image of a planet. "ArchAngel, your timing is spooky lately," said Eddie with a laugh.

Lance glanced over his shoulder. "That's Kezza, where the next mission will take place."

"The Brotherhood has been disbanded, correct?" asked Julianna.

"Yes, they have. Thousands of Brotherhood soldiers are being returned to Kezza in batches," said Lance.

"Then why is there a mission on Kezza?" asked Eddie. "It would appear that their problems have been solved."

"It would *appear*," repeated Lance. "However, when the Brotherhood enslaved its military force, it took away nearly a third of the population, especially in the north. As has happened in many times of war, those who were left behind were expected to take on all the responsibilities of the society. Our reports indicate that manufacturing, farming, and construction all took a hit when most of the male population was enlisted in the Brotherhood."

Jack turned to Julianna and Eddie. "Ghost Squadron is about defending the Federation, but also it's important that we help to rebuild—even those outside our borders. The Kezzin need our help."

"I couldn't agree more," stated Eddie.

Lance's mouth spread in a flat smile. "The returnees will need time to adapt after their ordeal. Many were brainwashed into serving or, like Lars, threatened. There are several areas which could use our help rebuilding, farming or simply offering a helping hand. This mission will support this area," he pointed to a portion of the northern continent on the map, "which has suffered due to Felix's silent war."

"Lars is from the north, right?" Julianna asked Eddie.

He thought for a moment, then nodded. "I believe so."

"I'm sure he will be anxious to assist your efforts, then," stated Lance.

8

Omega-line Q-Ship, Planet Kezza, Tangki System

It felt different to fly a full Q-Ship, filled with Special Ops soldiers. It felt *good*. The team was rowdy in the back, all of them pumped for the mission. After fighting Mamaths, a safe humanitarian mission was probably a vacation. That wasn't to say that the work on Kezza would be easy. Julianna knew that after reviewing the reports.

The north had suffered greatly, most of their crops for livestock dying and many of their buildings taking serious storm damage. Having lost nearly half of their population to the Brotherhood, they were underprepared for the annual storms. The females, children and elderly were given the burden of buckling down the infrastructure, which they did, but it wasn't enough.

The females did an incredible job of taking the extra responsibility of farming, production and general societal requirements. However, no population can flourish with only one sex. That was clear to Julianna after reviewing the reports. They both have their strengths and there is purpose between the yin and yang of every population. Take one and the other will suffer because the balance is off.

Julianna glanced at the men and women in the back of the Q-Ship. She felt that this balance had been achieved with Ghost Squadron.

Eddie's voice crackled over the comm. "Blackbeard to Carnivore."

"Carnivore here," said Lars. He was flying the older Q-Ship. Eddie had received the honor of flying the newest Q-Ship, which was identical to the one Julianna currently flew. However, Eddie also had Hatch sitting next to him, critically watching his every move.

"Where do you suppose the best place to land and set up camp is?" asked Eddie.

"The mountain ridge ahead provides cover from the desert winds that will sweep in at night," said Lars. "There are three nearby villages, so we won't have to travel far."

"Sounds good," said Eddie. "Lead the way, Carnivore. I'll have the Black Eagles drop supplies south of here, which should take care of that area."

"That's a good plan," said Lars.

Lars hadn't displayed the slightest micro-expression of excitement when told about this mission. Instead the Kezzin had simply nodded. Julianna knew he had to be brimming with emotion, returning to his home planet after everything. She wondered if he'd crack now that they were setting down on the planet. She wondered if she would in his position.

Eddie set the ship down so smoothly most would not have felt the landing.

Hatch wiped one of his tentacles across his forehead. "I thought you were going to make widows of all my wives."

Eddie looked at the Londil in confusion. "That landing wasn't up to your standards?"

"You call that a landing?" asked Hatch. "I think 'crash' is more accurate."

Eddie smiled. "Great job with this ship. She flies like a dream." He patted the controls affectionately.

"It would have been another week without Knox's help," said Hatch and then his eyes skirted to the back briefly where Knox sat alongside crates of supplies. *Did Hatch just give someone a compliment?* Eddie thought, trying to cover his shock. If Hatch thought he'd been too nice, then he'd probably make up for it with a bigger critique later.

Eddie unstrapped himself, popping up from his seat. "I'll get this unloaded. The rest of you go off to do what you do best."

Hatch regarded Eddie with a skeptical expression, a few quips probably scrolling through his head. Finally, he slipped from the seat made especially for him and waddled for the exit. "Grab the tool box, Gunner," he said to Knox, using the name the crew had affectionately given to him. He already had the bright yellow, oversized tool chest in his hands and an eager look on his face.

"Fletcher's team and the rest of us are going to do important stuff. But you two are here to offer the real help," said Eddie, proudly.

Hatch hesitated, his expression uncertain. "Well, thanks," he finally said, reluctance heavy in his tone. "I still think you fly like a space chimp."

"Of course you do. I'll work on it, Doc," said Eddie, offering the mechanic a wide grin.

Fletcher's team had dispersed at once, spreading out to the closest villages, offering help to any who needed it. A goodwill message had been sent ahead of time and was warmly received. The Kezzin hadn't always been friendly to humans, but suffering a great tragedy such as they had had changed things. There were still those who silently followed the Brotherhood and the pirates who ransacked human ships. However, most of the individual Kezzin were like Lars and simply wanted to live a simple life without the violence and power plays. The Kezzin were simple, Lars had told Eddie. They enjoyed the sun, outdoors, family, and the hunt.

Julianna approached Eddie with an uncertain expression on her face. He'd unloaded his supplies into the main area in record time. Well, record time for him. Fletcher's team grabbed the water and building supplies, ready to take them to the remote villages. They'd make repairs and assist the Kezzin long into the night. It was good for them. It was good for everyone.

"Why have you been giving me strange looks lately?" asked Eddie, crossing his arms on his chest and looking directly at Julianna.

"Define 'lately,'" she said. Her tone was serious, but

there was a playful smile on her face. "I've regarded you with disdain from the beginning."

Eddie whistled, shaking his head. "Disdain? I didn't realize I irritated you that much."

"Of course you don't. You had a shit-eating grin on your face as you worked."

Eddie rubbed his hand over his lips as if to confirm the smile on his face. "Oh, was I grinning? I hadn't realized."

"You always grin, but a bit more than usual today," observed Julianna.

"That's easy. I'm excited to be here. It isn't every day that we get to do something like this. Something that gives back."

"We risk our necks every damn day to fight bullies," argued Julianna.

Eddie shook his head. "But this is different. On those occasions we're stopping the bad guys, but here we're helping the good guys."

They looked out to where Fletcher's team were spread out in different directions, off to help the Kezzin villages.

"Yeah, I know what you meant. I was just giving you shit," said Julianna.

"I know. I can't imagine it any other way."

"Imagine what?" she asked. "Me, giving you shit?"

He grinned. "It's my constant. What can I say?"

Julianna pointed at Lar's Q-Ship, which still sat closed up. "You think he's coming out anytime soon or should we go in there and get him out?"

Eddie's eyes drifted to a large Kezzin who was approaching. He looked about like all Kezzin with their red scaly skin and pointy chin. However, this one had something different about him. "I think we're not going to have to," said Eddie.

The Kezzin had an expression that Eddie recognized. He was in confused disbelief. From the front of the Q-Ship, the alien could be seen. That's probably why a moment later the hatch finally opened and Lars stepped out, looking at the Kezzin like one does an old friend.

Hiraeth. That's the word that had been streaming through Lars Malseen's head for the last year. He was certain when the Brotherhood took him that he would never return home, or that Kezza would never exist like it was before. The word, hiraeth, he'd run across while reading, nearly falling to his knees when he looked up its meaning. "Homesickness for a place to which you cannot return, that maybe never was." Nostalgia didn't quite fit when Lars thought of Kezza. It didn't accurately describe the doom and regret he felt. *Hiraeth*, though…that word nailed it.

But here he was at last. Against all odds, Lars had returned. And before him was the face he'd thought he'd never see again.

"Dequan…" Lars choked on the name. The sun silhouetted his brother, casting him in dark shadows. Still he recognized that face. He'd know it anywhere.

"Lars," said Dequan, halting.

The brothers stood fifteen feet apart, unmoving. It had been nearly impossible for Lars to come out of the Q-Ship. He feared that his brother had been enlisted or harmed. He feared the worst. Not coming back to Kezza was almost easier than returning, after all this time.

The brothers stood fifteen feet apart, and Lars remained in place. He couldn't move. What if this were a dream? He'd dreamt this a thousand times, only to wake up and realize that he wasn't home and maybe never would be.

Dequan moved first. He strode forward with his head tilted like he wasn't sure he was seeing his brother correctly.

"Brother, you have returned. I knew you would," said Dequan when he was only a few feet away.

"I've wanted to for quite some time, but there was work to be done first. I couldn't come back until the Kezzin were safe from the Brotherhood." Now that Lars had started talking, it felt like he'd never stop. He wanted to bound forward and embrace his brother, but something still kept him rooted in place. Lars knew exactly what it was. It was his own fear. His own regret.

Dequan was regarding him like he was an alien. He was regarding him like he was different. Wrong, somehow. That's what Lars had feared. And here it was. The rejection.

"Did the Brotherhood…" Lars' question trailed away.

Dequan shook his head. "No, they didn't take me. I took the family to the mountains. We hid there, just as you told us to do."

Lars let out a breath of relief. "I'm glad for that. The battles were brutal. Many Kezzin were killed." His mind flashed to the lieutenant that he killed on Nexus. To the many Kezzin he had been forced to fight in defense of the Federation.

"You escaped the Brotherhood. That's what your letter said," said Dequan.

So he had *gotten the letter.* Had he pieced the rest together?

"Yes, and I joined Ghost Squadron. We fought the Brotherhood." Lars gestured toward Eddie and Julianna, who stood in the distance. Both looked away quickly, as if they weren't eavesdropping on the reunion. "It is because of the captain and the commander that the Brotherhood was disbanded and many Kezzin have returned home."

"You fought the Brotherhood? You fought your own?" asked Dequan.

Lars heart sank. He wanted to jump back into the Q-Ship and fly away, never to return to Kezza, but instead he dropped his gaze to the ground. "I did what I had to for the greater good."

"Did you kill Brotherhood soldiers?" asked Dequan. He had always challenged Lars, always pushed him until he told the truth. It had been like this since they were young.

"I did what I had to for the greater good," Lars repeated.

Dequan let out a heavy sigh. He covered his forehead and eyes with his hand, covering the new stress on his face.

"Yes, Dequan, I killed my own. I had to. I know you must hate me. My race will never accept me, but—"

"I don't hate you," said Dequan in disbelief. He dropped his hand, shaking his head. "I respect you more than ever, Lars."

"You do?" asked Lars, confused. This wasn't how he had expected it to go.

"Because of you and Ghost Squadron, our people are *free*," said Dequan, his tone overflowing with conviction. "Most wouldn't have escaped the Brotherhood. Only *you* did, as far as I can tell, and I know of no one else who would fight his own people to free them. You did what you had to because you, Lars, are an incredibly selfless person. You could have run or hidden, but instead you stood up to the leaders of the Brotherhood in order to bring them down."

Lars' mouth dropped open. His throat was suddenly dry, and his eyes couldn't blink. "You understand, then?"

"Perfectly," said Dequan, "and I couldn't be prouder of you, brother."

Suddenly Lars' feet unstuck from the ground, and he nearly lost his balance. He wrapped his arms around his brother. This was the moment he couldn't believe would happen—and yet it had, here and now. Lars pressed his eyes shut, breathing deeply.

Maybe you *could* go home...and find that your heart had never left.

9

Village of Gazer, Planet Kezza, Tangki System

"Here's your problem," said Hatch, pulling a long bolt out of the top of a combine. The Kezzin around him all nodded like this made perfect sense. In the distance the crops that fed the herds had been almost completely decimated. Apparently, the storms had been the first assault and then a fungus took out most of rest of the field. The pastures were filled with Kezzin and humans who were trying to replant it.

Hatch wiped the grease from his tentacles with a rag, then stepped down from the machine. "How's the irrigation system?" he asked Knox, who was bent over with his head inside a box buried in the ground.

Knox straightened up with dirt on his nose and cheeks, and smiled. "Let's find out. Are you ready?"

Hatch pinned two tentacles to his sides and deflated his cheeks. "No, I'd like to melt in this heat for a few more hours."

"Oh, okay. Never mind, then." Knox laughed.

"Go on. Let's see if you've learned anything I taught you or you're as obtuse as the crew on *ArchAngel*," said Hatch.

"But if it works then all those in the field will get wet. Shouldn't we warn them first?"

"You're real confident, aren't you?" asked Hatch.

"Well, no. It's just a precaution," said Knox, his eyes dropping to the dry ground. "I'm sure it won't work. Not the first time at least. I did everything you told me to do, but I probably screwed something up."

"Then you have nothing to worry about and no one will get wet. Go on then," said Hatch, urging Knox by waving one of his tentacles in the air over his head.

Knox nodded, reaching into the box. He flipped a series of switches. Then he stood up and looked out at the field with uncertainty. Nothing happened. As if confirming his suspicions of failure, he nodded. "Yeah, I figured I hadn't connected the—"

A gentle mist streamed from the irrigation hoses that snaked through the field. Those planting jumped with alarm, many of them darting out of the field. The hoses hiccupped several times, but the flow of water continued steady and strong.

Hatch laughed as the field cleared out. "Blame the kid. It's his fault you all got a shower," he said to the workers racing in their direction. He looked at Knox with a sort of smile on his face. "Good work, Gunner. That irrigation system is going to really help this crop to recover."

"Thanks," said Knox, his pale cheeks glowing pink. "I just followed your instructions."

"Well, I can't do everything myself, now can I?" Hatch

said, grimacing at a pair who were pushing a tractor in their direction. "Oh hell, they have another one for us to repair. No rest for the brilliant, and the dumb don't need any."

Knox's head was under the hood of the old tractor when he heard the familiar laugh. He pulled his head up to spy the person he thought the laughter belonged to. However, Lars' face was brighter than he'd ever seen it.

Lars had knelt, and was looking up at a young Kezzin. Knox supposed the child was his niece, and the pair behind her Lars' family. So badly did Knox want to be happy for his friend. He'd read the hesitation in him when they were preparing to come to Kezza. Knox realized that returning to his home planet had been difficult for Lars. Knox couldn't relate.

He'd never had a home to return to, not really. He and his Pops had moved around a lot since the beginning, but he'd never understood why. And then one day, Knox's Pops had suddenly disappeared. He didn't go to the store and not come back or anything like that. Literally, one moment he was there, in the other room, and then he was gone. There was no explanation, which is why after a week, Knox fled, an unsettling feeling in his chest.

That feeling had never disappeared. He didn't know if it ever would. Something told him that if he ever found out the truth, then maybe it would. But that was a desperate hope because how does one find a man who vanished with zero clues?

A tentacle waved in front of Knox's face. "Hey, who gave you a break?" asked Hatch.

Knox shook his head slightly and spun to face Hatch. He'd been staring at nothing for who-knew-how-long. His thoughts had taken over, gotten to him. That didn't happen when he worked, made things.

"Sorry, Doctor A'Din Hatcherik," said Knox, his face flushing hot. He'd just gotten praise from Hatch, and then a moment later was caught goofing off. *Damn it.*

Hatch's gaze followed where Knox had been staring, and he blinked at the Kezzin family reunion before looking at the tractor. "Why don't you go grab something to drink? It's easy to get dehydrated on this lizard planet."

"No, I'm good. I'll get back to work," said Knox quickly, leaning forward intently to replace the spark plugs in the old tractor.

"That wasn't a request. It was an order, Gunner," said Hatch, his voice strict. "You're no use to me if you get yourself sick."

Knox's gaze, without his permission, shot back to Lars' family. He had his arm around his brother's shoulder, and a look of pure happiness on his face. Knox nodded, backing away. "Okay. I'll be back in a few, though."

"Take your time, kid," said Hatch. He turned to the Kezzin and the Federation crew working around them. "Why don't you lot clear off? We can't work with all of you clogging up this space."

Those around the field retreated at Hatch's order, Lars and his family included.

10

Intelligence Center, QBS *ArchAngel*, Behemoth System

Chester rocked his head back and forth. Timbaland was a freaking genius. The new music coming out of Onyx Station didn't compare. He preferred to listen to the *Shock Value* album rather than the techno crap in the background of the first-person shooter game he was playing.

Chester jerked to the side as if he were dodging the attack on the screen.

"No you don't, sucker," he yelled at the screen, firing off several rounds at the scoundrels he was fighting.

Swaying his shoulders to the music, Chester rocked his head and sang.

He chanced a glance at Harley who was looking up at him like expecting a treat. "You're right, Har, these are some sweet, sweet moves."

Behind him, Marilla giggled.

He paused the game and spun around. "Oh, have you decided to quit pretending to ignore me."

"I'm not ignoring you. Or pretending to do so," she argued. Well, she lied. He'd caught her eyeing him in the mirror he'd positioned beside his front monitor. The mirror was a new addition, but he was certain her glances at his back wasn't anything new. Or at least he hoped not.

"I know, I'm pretty distracting," said Chester, picking up his shirt off his shoulders. "If it's ever too much for you and your crazy work ethic, let me know."

"Do you think I want to be relocated to a different work area? Maybe on the bridge?" asked Marilla with a playful smile on her face.

"Oh, heck nah. I'll just quiet down. That tech support geek already moved out of here because of my antics. I get that I'm a bit much," said Chester. He'd laid it on pretty thick when that dork had been in the office with them. He'd planned all along to get him to request a different workstation, leaving only Marilla and Chester in the Intelligence Center.

"You don't have to worry. You don't distract me. I actually find you pretty entertaining," said Marilla, and motioned to Harley. "It appears he does too."

"Well, good." He spun back and resumed playing the game.

"What is this?" asked the captain.

Chester spun around to find Eddie standing in the doorway. He was right on time, probably having gotten his meeting request as soon as he returned from Kezza.

"I know, he's blatantly playing games on the job. You should fire him and then throw him out the airlock," said Marilla dryly.

Eddie shot a look of surprise at the communication officer. "Damn, when did you get so feisty?"

"I believe it's my influence," stated Chester.

"Well, maybe I need to split you two up," joked Eddie. "I can't have you corrupting our sweet Marilla."

"I've got you all fooled," said Marilla, stretching to a standing position. "I've always been this way. You all mistake my quiet nature for niceness."

"Oh, well, it's not hard to fool me," said Eddie with a laugh. He looked at Chester, his eyes wide on the paused game on the big screen. "And I'm not firing this guy. Instead, I want you to allow me to play. What is this?"

Marilla chuckled, slapping her hand on her leg to get Harley's attention. The dog perked up and trotted over. "I figured you wouldn't fire Chest. There's no way you could replace him." She left without another word, and Harley followed her.

Eddie watched her leave and then turned to Chester. "You guys are cute."

"Like a couple of kittens curled up in front of a fire," said Chester.

"Yeah, about like that," said Eddie, reaching over and picking up the wireless controller sitting on Chester's desk. "All right, I got to play this. Can I?"

"Knock yourself out," said Chester, leaning back in his chair with his hands behind his head. "I'll go ahead and tell you what I found out while you play, which I'll warn you only begs for more questions."

Eddie gave Chester a sideways skeptical look before unpausing the game. "I don't like the sound of that."

"Yeah, well, unfortunately I found just enough information to ask a dozen more questions." Chester watched as Eddie took a fatal hit. He started a new game, tapping the controls hard with frustration.

"Go on then," said Eddie.

"You're a busy man so I'll sum this up for you as best I can," began Chester. "There is some sort of weapon that Felix has created. I have no idea what it is or who developed it, although I'm continuing to follow leads."

"When not gaming," added Eddie.

"Exactly," said Chester, firing a finger at him. "What I found tells me that there's one sure fire way to determine what this thing is."

"Call the guy up and ask him?" joked Eddie, taking another hit. He was much better at live combat than the virtual kind, thank goodness.

"Yeah, you could do that, but I doubt he'll tell you. I've been hacking all sorts of his systems, but hitting major firewalls. What I need is direct access to his personal accounts," said Chester.

"Which we get…how?" asked Eddie.

"By going aboard *Unsurpassed*," said Chester, brandishing a clever grin at the captain.

Eddie lowered the controls with an utterly confused expression on his face. "You're kidding, right?"

Chester grimaced when Eddie was obliterated in the game. "I'm not kidding. My jokes are way better than that. I know it sounds farfetched, but I've been playing with the idea and think it's a good one. Risky, yes, but solid."

"You think because I'm enhanced I'll go for something so insane, don't you?" asked Eddie, restarting the game once more.

"I think you're a man who wants solutions to problems. Our problem is that we don't know what Felix has. All we can confirm is that he had something commissioned, my digging has told me that much, anyway."

"And if we get aboard *Unsurpassed* and grant you access to his system, you think you can find what we're looking for?" asked Eddie.

"I know that I can," said Chester, proudly.

"There's the whole problem that we could get caught, going onboard an enemy ship and all," said Eddie, tapping the button on the control repeatedly.

"Believe me, a major concern for me. I don't even have any combat experience, unless gaming counts," said Chester.

"It doesn't," said Eddie, dropping the control down for a second time. "And you need to go on this suicide mission yourself? Explain."

"The last time I checked, you're good with a gun, but you can't hack into a computer system to save your life," said Chester.

"Why thank you. And no, I don't think I can," said Eddie. "I thought you said that if we got aboard *Unsurpassed* we'd have access to the records."

"True, we'll have access, but they'll still be protected. You're going to need someone skilled that can disable their security and hack into the system," said Chester.

"Okay, that would be you," said Eddie and then he grunted when he got killed yet again. He dropped the controls on the desk in front of Chester. "All right, so any ideas on how we're going to stroll aboard *Unsurpassed* and hack into the systems?"

Chester picked up the control and started a new game. "Strategy is for you and the commander to figure out. You get me in there and I'll get what you need."

Eddie watched for a long few seconds as Chester wasted a few of the digital enemies with ease. "All right, chief. I'll go and mull this over with Julianna. Keep doing what you're doing. You're brilliant at it."

Chester took out a sniper and smiled broadly. "You got it, boss."

11

Cargo Bay, QBS *ArchAngel,* Behemoth System

"Don't cry, it's only a knock-knock joke," said Pip overhead as Eddie entered the cargo bay. Hatch gave Knox a classic deadpan look to which the young mechanic simply shook his head. "Get it! Boo-who. Don't cry." Pip laughed loudly at his own joke.

Eddie shot a curious glance at Julianna. She shrugged and gave him a "You don't want to know" look.

"Okay, I've got another one," said Pip overhead.

"I'm fairly certain we've had our fill," said Julianna. "Teach is here and we have to discuss the next mission with him."

"I'll make it fast," said Pip, ignoring her. "Knock-knock."

Julianna stared at Hatch, who waddled away, shaking a wrench above his head.

When no one said anything, Eddie said, "Who is there?"

"Little old lady," answered Pip.

Eddie grinned, but the other three didn't at all look

impressed. They'd obviously been suffering from these jokes for too long. "Little old lady who?"

"Nice! I didn't know you could yodel," chirped Pip. "*Ba-dum-tss!*"

Eddie narrowed his eyes. "I don't get it."

"None of us do," said Julianna, waving him over.

"Captain, will you remember me in an hour?" asked Pip.

Even more confused, Eddie shook his head. "Of course, you strange AI."

"Shush it, Pip. We have real work to do," said Julianna, her tone punishing.

"All work and no play makes Julianna a—"

"Can Pip be reprogrammed now that he's a true AI?" she asked Hatch, cutting Pip off.

Hatched puffed his cheeks. "Certainly. I'm considering changing his software as we speak."

Eddie laughed at the absurdity of all this. Pip was good for the crew, more lately than ever before. "I heard you mention the mission. You received the report from Chester? Did you *flip*? Pretty gnarly idea, huh?"

"It's brilliant," said Julianna, to his surprise. "That's why I came here to meet with Hatch. However, we have another problem."

"Of course we do. Lay it on me," said Eddie.

Hatch cleared his throat, scuttling forward. He and Knox appeared to be building the next Q-Ship. "Sneaking onto *Unsurpassed* is a very doable mission, in my mind. However, in order to be successful, you're going to need cloaking technology."

"Yeah, I was thinking we'd use the personal cloaking belts again," said Eddie.

"Yes, that would be the right approach. However, our crystal supply has been depleted. I used the rest of them when we created the last Q-Ship," muttered Hatch, his attention half on the framework of the ship sitting before them. "We're going to need more of the aether crystals if I'm going to keep building these ships, but also for any additional personal cloaks."

Eddie nodded. "Tell us what you need us to do."

"I tried placing an order for them, but it's going to be several months," said Hatch.

"Several *months*?" asked Julianna with alarm. "We can't wait that long. Felix is up to something."

"I figured you couldn't. Also, the orders keep getting backlogged, so I'm guessing something is wrong on the mining end. I suspect as much at least, based on what I know about where they come from," said Hatch.

"What about it?" asked Eddie.

"They can only be mined from a single planet called Berosia. It's an incredibly underdeveloped world way out on the frontier," said Hatch.

"We're used to that sort of thing," said Eddie. "So you need us to buzz over there and mine you some crystals, is that right?"

"I wish it were that simple. Mining isn't an easy operation. It involves explosives," said Hatch.

"Why didn't you lead with that?" asked Eddie. "I'm all over this."

"I understand that Lieutenant Fletcher has someone on his team who is skilled with explosive ordinance," said Julianna.

"Yeah, they needed those to fight the Mamaths," said

Eddie, nodding.

"You're going to need Fletcher's team," cut in Hatch. "That's the other piece of this. I suspect that the reason the crystals are on backorder is that the planet is overrun with pirates. They know that the aether is highly valuable and many of them go to great lengths to steal and sell them on the black market."

"Fight some pirates and steal some cloaking crystals," said Eddie, slapping his hands together. "We can do all that. Then you'll have what you need to make our personal cloaking devices?"

Hatch nodded, his gaze back on the Q-Ship as he drifted off into deep concentration.

"Captain?" asked Pip.

"Yes?" answered Eddie.

"Will you remember me in a day?" asked Pip.

"Of course, buddy," said Eddie, giving Julianna a curious look. "What's with these questions?"

"Knock-knock," said Pip.

Eddie couldn't help but chuckle. "Okay, I'll indulge you one last time. Who's there?"

"What? You've forgotten me already!" said Pip, laughing at his own joke.

Alpha-line Q-Ship, Berosia Airspace, Davida System

Berosia wasn't an easy planet to get to, making the crystals even more valuable. The QBS *ArchAngel* had to gate twice, and still the planet was a good way off.

"I think we should consider jumping back to the ship," said Julianna to Eddie.

He read the hesitation in her voice. "You're worried we're going to run into trouble?"

"I'm betting on it, based on past experience," said Julianna. "Carnivore, this is Strong Arm. Do you copy?"

The comm clicked several times before Lars' voice came over it. "Copy, Strong Arm. I'm right behind you."

When given the option to stay on Kezza, Lars declined immediately. He said he'd enjoyed reconnecting with his family, but his duty was with Ghost Squadron. Since then, he'd appeared lighter, like a great burden had been lifted from his shoulders. Julianna suspected that many of his demons had been buried on Kezza, all for the better.

"I see that," said Julianna. "We're landing on the eastern side of the mountain straight ahead."

The planet of Berosia was as Hatch had described it—completely undeveloped. It reminded Julianna of Sagano, with its thick forests and tropical climate.

"The mountain that looks like a lady's face," said Eddie, apparently trying to clarify. There was a row of mountains ahead.

"A human lady or a Kezzin female?" joked Lars.

"Since she has a round nose and smooth cheeks, I'm going with 'human lady,'" said Eddie.

"I see the one you're talking about. You humans sure are ugly," said Lars.

"Right back at you, buddy," said Eddie.

"All is clear for landing," said Pip overhead. "I've scouted and founded no evidence of pirate activity."

"Well, maybe the good doctor was overly cautious and worried over nothing," said Eddie. He turned around, looking at Lieutenant Fletcher. "Have your team on high-alert anyway. Pirates are masters at hiding and those trees could be covering a lot.

"Yes sir," said Fletcher. "I suspect you're right."

Julianna set the Q-Ship down at the base of the mountain, in a clearing of sorts. She watched the radar as Lars did the same thing. He was carrying the other half of Fletcher's team, as well as a few rounds of the explosive. The supply had been divided up, for obvious reasons.

Julianna stood up and looked at the lieutenant. This was their first real mission together. She and Eddie weren't used to having a team of soldiers, and although it was supposed to make their job easier, it also made it more complicated.

"Comms up?" asked Julianna.

There was a collective yes from the ship.

"Lieutenant, the captain and I are going to go in first to survey the area. Wait for our orders," said Julianna.

He nodded his consent. "We'll be ready and waiting."

"Great," replied Julianna and then her gaze fell to the floor of the Q-Ship. "Carnivore, I want you with the Q-Ships. We need to be in position to make a fast get away if something happens. Do you copy?"

"Copy, Strong Arm," answered Lars. "I'll keep visual from this location."

"Very good," said Julianna, securing her weapons. Seriously, they needed better guns. After mining a bunch of cloaking crystals, their next mission needed to be to steal real weapons. Maybe if they encountered any pirates on this trip they'd have something decent they could confiscate.

"All right, ready to roll out," imparted Eddie, giving her an excited look.

"Let's go and see what this planet is all about," said Julianna.

A hot wind hit Eddie's face when they disembarked from the Q-Ship. Whereas Sagano was covered in flat lands and forests, Berosia was uneven terrain and littered with tall peaks.

"Up for a hike?" asked Eddie, looking up at the steep jaunt ahead. According to Hatch, this was the location for a large crop of the crystals.

"Why is it so quiet?" asked Julianna, looking around, worry on her face.

"Why are you always fretting? Maybe there aren't any pirates. Maybe Hatch was being overly concerned," said Eddie.

Julianna scanned the tropical forest where they stood, an uncertain look on her face. "I don't know. Something doesn't feel right about this place. There's no noise."

"No noise is good, me thinks," said Eddie, his laugh loud in the silent forest.

"I don't know," Julianna repeated. "Let's get up to that ridge and to the mouth of the first set of caves. From up there we might get a better idea of what's going on here."

"And remember that it could be nothing. There're thousands of mountains on this planet, all rich with these crystals. We might have chosen an untapped one," said Eddie.

"Which is why there's a clear trail all the way up there?" asked Julianna sarcastically.

"Good point, Fregin. Never mind. We're probably screwed," said Eddie.

"Probably," agreed Julianna, setting off first.

The hill… Well, it wasn't really a hill. The mountain—the giant steep-ass mountain—sloped straight up, requiring the pair to lean forward and use their hands to secure their balance several times. If Julianna and Eddie, both enhanced individuals, were having this much trouble hiking up to this cave, Eddie thought it was unlikely that pirates could do it on a good day.

He observed that Julianna wasn't out of breath, although the hike *was* taking a toll. This was the first time he had seen her break a sweat.

She straightened slightly and looked at the valley below. They'd only been hiking a short while and already gone up a couple thousand feet in elevation, which gave them a killer view.

"Q-Ships look like little ants down there," said Eddie.

"They sure do." Julianna nodded over to a wide ledge below them. "Maybe we should have parked the ships right there."

He laughed. "Yeah, but then we wouldn't have gotten in this amazing hike."

"True, but my concern is for the team," said Julianna. "If it took us this much effort to get up the mountain, just think about how long it will take them."

Static filled the comm for a moment. "Fletcher here. You worried us normal humans are going to hold you back?"

"We're banking on it," said Eddie. "And Strong Arm is right. This mountain is a bitch. Pip and Lars, can you relocate the ships here? Keep them cloaked, though, since they'll be in the wide open."

"Copy, Blackbeard," said Lars. "I'll follow behind Pip."

Eddie looked to Julianna, sweat beading on his forehead. "Good call, Commander. You're always thinking."

"Thank—"

Shots from below sprayed the side of the mountain, making both duck down at once. Gravel and rock flew up from the attack. Out in the wide open, there was nowhere for Julianna and Eddie to go except for up, away from the assault.

"We're under attack," whispered Julianna, moving faster than before. "Fletcher, we need your team on as back up now."

"We're in transport. We'll be on the ground in—"

"Twenty seconds," said Lars, completing Fletcher's sentence.

Shots from overhead fired into the tree from the cloaked Q-Ships.

"We've got you covered," said Pip over the comm.

Shots fired from the mouth of the cave zoomed right past their heads. Eddie dove onto Julianna, knocking her flat to the ground. From on top of her, he covered his head from the oncoming bullets.

"We have enemy fire from the cave," said Julianna.

"I'm on it," said Lars. "Pip, take care of the forest floor."

"We need those Q-Ships on the ground. We're stranded over here," yelled Eddie, his face pressed into Julianna's.

"My team is jumping out right now," said Fletcher. "Pip needs to be able to maneuver."

Eddie pushed up off of Julianna when all he could hear was the firing from the Q-Ships. She gave him a strange look—relief mixed with awkwardness. "Sorry if I invaded your personal space. Didn't want to see holes in you."

"Thanks. I'll survive the trespassing," said Julianna, taking the hand he offered her. She swiveled her head over her shoulder, eying the cave.

"Do you think you got them, Carnivore?" asked Eddie.

"Hard to tell," said Lars. "We'll cover your backs from here."

"My team is on the ground," said Fletcher over the comm, but Eddie could clearly see them as they moved ahead, guns at the ready.

"Whoever was firing has either been shot down or has retreated," said Fletcher.

"Or they're waiting to ambush us when we get up there," said Julianna.

Fletcher agreed with a nod. He yanked a grenade from the side of his arm and pulled out the pin. Then he threw it toward the mouth of the cave, a good distance from the group. Everyone covered their heads at once, bracing for the explosion. It rocked the mountain a moment later, making many lose their footing.

Through the dust of the explosion, Julianna said, "You think blowing up the cave is a good idea? What if you block our entrance?"

"Then I'll blow us up a new one," said Fletcher, his voice

light and calm in the face of all this danger. Eddie instantly liked the guy more. It was easy to keep ones cool on a regular basis, but to do so when in battle was impressive. It was the mark of a true soldier.

"You're the explosive expert, so whatever you say," said Julianna.

"I appreciate that," said Fletcher, motioning to a few of his team members who had explosives strapped to their back. Carrying them into the mountain was a dangerous job, but Fletcher's team had nearly fought over the responsibility. "You three, I want you to spread out. Don't clump together in case one of your explosives gets triggered."

They all nodded at once.

"Commander, you ready to see who's waiting for us?" asked Eddie.

"Yes, and let's hope the gunfire was a mistake. Otherwise we'll hand them their asses on a fucking silver platter," said Julianna.

"With a side of fries and a cold beer," said Eddie. Oh, that sounded so good right then it made his stomach give a lurch. He rubbed his abdomen. *Just wait,* he told himself.

Lady Face Mountain, Planet Berosia, Davida System

Scurrying down low, Julianna sped up the last bit of scree, throwing her back against the front of the cave. Eddie followed suit, meeting her on the other side. Fletcher's team were stationed down lower, crouched close to the rock-strewn ground.

"Fire on the ground has ceased," said Lars over the comm. "We will stay on alert."

Julianna didn't answer. Instead she peered around into the mouth of the cave. It was dark and smelled of minerals and dank. Only a few feet away were the bodies of three Kezzins. Pirates by the look of their dress and shitty guns.

She kicked the nearest pistol away right as Eddie joined her. He leaned down and checked the bodies.

"Dead," he said, standing.

"It's their own damn fault. We just came to grab a few crystals. No one had to die," said Julianna.

"When have you ever known pirates to share?" asked

Eddie surveying the rest of the cave from where they stood.

"I guess I believe people will change," she said, her tone coated in condescension.

"No, you don't. Otherwise you'd be a therapist and not a soldier," said Eddie.

"Can't put anything past you," said Julianna as Fletcher arrived beside the pair.

"I have one of my snipers hidden in the trees. She'll assist the ships with clearing out the pirates below," said Fletcher.

"Great," said Eddie, breathing deeply. "Now we just have to get through these pirate-infested tunnels."

"Luckily Hatch provided us an option," said Julianna. She reached into her pack and pulled out a small drone, about the size of the palm of her hand. It was, of course equipped with a camera, but in a dark cave, that would provide little help. She fired the drone up and it rose into the air, sending out sonar pulses immediately. This told the device about the space around it and where it was free to fly. Julianna nudged the drone which hovered directly in front of her and it shot forward, flying down the open cave that disappeared into blackness.

Also from her pack, she retrieved a radar screen. Currently it had a single blue light, which told the location of the drone.

"It knows to keep flying forward, right?" asked Eddie.

"Correct," said Julianna. "It's a scouting drone so it won't retreat until we call it back."

"Or it gets blown up," said Eddie.

"Which will give Hatch yet another reason to want you dead," said Julianna.

"It wouldn't be right if he didn't despise me just a little bit," said Eddie as a red light blinked on the screen.

"Found one," said Julianna, eyeing the screen. "Looks like the next pirate isn't too far ahead."

"Why do you have to assume it's a pirate?" joked Eddie.

"Well, it could be Little Red Riding Hood and she's lost as fuck, but I'm going to go with pirate," said Julianna.

Another red dot blinked on the screen.

"Think we just found Grandma," said Eddie.

"Two pirates," Fletcher said, sounding confident. "My team can handle that if you want to stay here and send back surveillance from the drone."

At once, a blanket of red dots consumed half the radar. Ten to fifteen of them.

"I don't think that's Red and grandma after all," said Eddie.

"I'm guessing that's a large cave room where they are mining," said Julianna.

Eddie nodded.

The radar screen suddenly fell dark.

"What happened?" asked Fletcher.

"It appears they know we're here and spying," said Eddie.

"Which means we need to get a move on it before they have time to react," said Julianna. "Let's try for diplomacy and if that doesn't work we hand them their ass."

"In a doggy bag," added Eddie.

"We're going in first." Julianna gestured to herself and

Eddie. "Fletcher, keep your team on our heels. Explosives stay here until we clear the pirates."

"Yes, Commander," said Fletcher, retreating to convey the orders to his men.

Julianna gazed over at Eddie, who looked like a kid on Christmas morning. "You know the plan. Let's move out."

<hr>

Together, Eddie and Julianna moved soundlessly through the darkened cave. Their enhanced vision made it so they could make out the curve of the walls and the slope of the ground. An ambient light shone ahead giving them all they needed to sneak through the caves. Conversely, Fletcher's team would be carrying flashlights, but they were still at the entrance of the cave.

The noises of footsteps and whispering echoed ahead. Eddie halted at a bend in the tunnel, sure that the pirates were stationed just head. He pulled a small blue marble from his pocket. He was certain he would have to use this, but he'd agreed to try Julianna's approach first.

"We come in peace," she began, her voice clear and loud. The noise in the cave area ahead halted. Eddie could have sworn he heard the Kezzin all hold their breath.

"We aren't here to fight. We've come for a supply of aether crystals. That's all," continued Julianna.

There was a loud laugh. "You're mistaken, human. This is not your mountain and you aren't wanted here."

"Give us a supply of aether and we will leave then," said Julianna. She was poised, her tone full of strength. It was impressive, although Eddie still didn't think this would work. Negotiating with pirates was a nasty business.

This time many of the Kezzin laughed together, a sound like wood being sawed. "Do you have any idea how much these crystals are worth?"

"Yes, because we've tried to buy them, but pirates have apparently overrun the market," yelled Julianna, her tone finally full of heat.

Bullets sprayed past them, knocking into the cave wall beside them, chipping away at it. Julianna took a step back, disappointment on her face.

"We're under fire again," said Lars over the comm. "It's coming from the top of the mountain as well as from the forest floor."

"Same here," said Eddie. "Hold your position!"

He looked to Julianna and she consented to his silent question with a nod.

He twisted the grenade in his fingers and threw it around the bend. A moment later, he heard a loud snap, followed by a slight jolt that rocked the nearby area.

More bullets whizzed past them. The pirates had moved closer.

Eddie pulled another stun grenade from his pocket, activating and throwing it in less than a moment. Julianna darted out, firing as she moved. She ducked behind a large stalagmite, taking cover. Gunfire showered back, although Eddie could see that Julianna had gotten one of the nearest pirates who was out of range of the grenade.

From the mouth of the cave he could hear another battle being waged. Gunfire and explosions echoed through the tunnel.

"Can we limit the explosions, since we're in the belly of this beast?" yelled Eddie over the comm.

"Those are enemy bombs!" said Fletcher.

"Knock them out before they get us trapped in here!" snapped Julianna.

"Nona is trying to find the cause," said Fletcher, referring to his best sniper.

Shuffling feet told Eddie that they had a runner. The stun grenades obviously hadn't hit all the pirates. He pulled another blue marble from his pocket right as Julianna yelled, "He's too close!"

She whipped around the large stalagmite, firing a spray of bullets. The runner collapsed, sliding to a full stop, his head buried in the dirt. A moment later, Julianna stood tall, looking out at the open tunnel ahead. The enemy responded with several shots.

Julianna pressed the trigger and fired another barrage into the darkness, striking several unseen enemies in the process and filling the cave with maddening screams. A moment later, she stopped, and a smooth calm settled over the newly christened battleground.

Eddie peeled around the corner to find the area covered in smoke and Kezzin bodies. Most were passed out from the stun grenades. They wouldn't be conscious for at least an hour, although the technology was a bit inaccurate. The rest had been taken out by Julianna—all sixteen of them.

"Fletcher, we need a few of your team in here to secure these pirates," said Eddie, moving around the bodies.

"Copy," said Fletcher. "I'm headed that way. Nona took out the source at the top of the mountain."

"Good work," said Julianna, her voice little more than a whisper.

Shots fired at them from the side of the large room.

"Bastards just refuse to go quietly, don't they?" Eddie ducked down, trying to get a read on where the bullets were coming from.

From their position he could make out some of the cave room, but only enough to tell that the walls and ceiling were covered in purple crystals. The aether.

Julianna waved to get Eddie's attention and pointed up at a raised platform, a make-shift scaffolding.

Eddie saw what she meant. Far on the opposite side of the room, and quite exposed and perched at the top was a single Kezzin, rifle held at the ready.

Taking a deep breath, Eddie lifted his weapon and fired once. The pirate tumbled forward, falling hard on the cave floor below.

"I think that's all of them," said Eddie stepping away from the wall and further into the middle of the cave.

The pirates looked to have done the work for them. Crates of aether crystals lined one wall. From the look of the tools the pirates were using, they were sawing the crystals from the ceiling. How long must that take? Much longer than they had time for. But now they had a supply, if they stole this from the pirates. Julianna had tried to strike a deal with these guys. Too bad for them.

Behind them Fletcher and a few of his team arrived. He halted, taking in the eerie glow of the purple room. The crystals twinkled in the light, like a series of mirrors creating prisms all over the ceiling.

"I brought the explosives," said Fletcher, indicating to a

reinforced pack on his back. Two of his men went to work restraining the pirates stationed around the cave.

"We're not going to need that, it looks like," said Eddie pointing to the supply of crystals.

"Oh, wow," said Fletcher. "That just made our job a whole lot easier."

The floor of the cave rumbled a bit, making each of them freeze.

"I thought you said Nona took out the pirates on top," said Julianna.

"She did," said Fletcher. "Maybe that's a new batch of pirates with explosives." Fletcher clicked the comm box on his belt, switching the channel. "Nona, you have a new target?"

A confused expression fell on Fletcher's face. He looked over to Eddie and Julianna. "She says that it's all quiet up there."

The ground rumbled again. "Then what the fuck is that?" asked Julianna.

"How about we not find out," said Eddie. "Grab the stock and let's get the fuck out of here."

"The crates over here are full," said Julianna, pointing to a set of small wooden boxes on the other side of the cave room. All the crates were small, about the size of a shoe boxes. Eddie guessed that the crystals couldn't be packed in too tightly or they'd be damaged.

"Okay, let's get those in case we can't make another trip back," said Eddie, darting in that direction.

"You two," said Fletcher to his men restraining the passed out pirates. "Grab these crates over here. We don't have time to worry about those guys."

The men dropped the pirates they'd been binding and ran for the crates.

Eddie learned that the small shoe box-sized crates were surprisingly heavy. That must have been another reason they were packed in small containers. He groaned when he tried to lift the box. It felt like it was full of lead, even using his enhanced strength. The soldiers heaved at the boxes, not displacing them at first, making it look glued to the ground.

"Fucking heavy, huh?" asked Eddie.

"You're not kidding," said Fletcher, letting out a loud breath as he awkwardly adjusted a crate in his arms.

"Is it?" asked Julianna, turning. She had two of the crates in her arms, stacked on top of each other.

"Fuck! How are you doing that?" asked Eddie. "We're both enhanced."

"I eat my veggies," said Julianna with a smirk. "And I've been enhanced a hell of a lot longer than you. Never forget that."

"Noted," said Eddie, breathing heavy under the strain of simply holding the crate.

The ground floor rumbled again, this time more violently than before.

"Oh, that doesn't seem good," said Eddie.

In the center of the room the ground splintered, dust and rock flying upward. The walls began to shake too.

Julianna set her crates down and pushed the men back into a new tunnel at the back of the room. "Get in there," she yelled, her head swiveling up nervously to the ceiling. Crystals, as if on cue, sprinkled down, but only a few. They burst into splinters of purple rain all over the cave room.

"Good call, Jules," said Eddie, watching the room change before their eyes.

The ground continued to quake, but mostly in the center of the cave. Large bits of stalagmites and rock exploded into the air, creating a heavy shower.

What burst out of the ground was unlike anything Eddie had ever seen.

1 3

Lady Face Mountain, Planet Berosia, Davida System

From the rock and debris, a giant worm monster emerged, violently writhing back and forth. Julianna stared up at it, stunned for a brief moment. It rose high into the air, its flat mouth screaming so loud that Julianna had to cover her ears. The guys around her dropped their crates and did the same. It wasn't just a high-pitched scream but also a noise that made her insides ache, like the sound carried a great sorrow with it.

The worm monster was as big around as a large tree, its skin a sickly gray, and lined with wrinkles. It continued to shift back and forth like it was in great pain.

"What the fuck is that?!" snapped Eddie, having to yell to be heard over the other screaming.

Julianna could hardly hear him. Hell, she could barely hear Pip, and he was in her head.

You've...ot...to...et...out...there, said Pip, his voice sounding frantic.

I know. How could something be so loud that she couldn't even hear the voice in her own head? The screeching was too much. She pressed harder into her ears. Turning for the tunnel where they stood, she saw only blackness. *Is there a way out if we follow the tunnel?*

Julianna retreated a few steps so she could focus more on Pip's voice.

It leads down, then dead-ends. It appears that it's been burrowed completely, probably by whatever is making that sound.

It's this animal. Do you know what it is? asked Julianna.

It's angry, but I can't say what it is yet, specifically. Try making it shut up so that I can think, said Pip.

I'll try. Figure out an option for us.

Julianna ran back to where Eddie and the others stood. The worm monster froze just as she arrived. It was like a statue, holding straight up in the air.

"Maybe this has been a complete misunderstanding and it's about to leave," whispered Eddie.

Fletcher and his men, looking relieved to have silence once more, nodded.

Get out of there! Now! Pip's voice seemed to echo in Julianna's.

What is it? The worm's frozen and gone silent.

Which means you're in trouble. That's a vermis rex. Pip said this like it should carry a great warning with it.

What's that?

A scream, louder and higher pitched than before ripped from the worm, cutting the silence. The scream ended as abruptly as it had started. Then it rhythmically lowered down until its giant end was facing the five. From the ground it looked like a puckered mouth, of sorts. The body of the giant worm vibrated, sending a shiver down Julianna's back.

"Guns at the ready!" she yelled.

Everyone already had their rifles up, but aimed them at the worm monster that floated several yards from the tunnel entrance. Then it opened its mouth to reveal a cavernous inside coated with row after row of triangular teeth.

A shriek that somehow burned Julianna's insides cut through the air.

"Fire," she exclaimed, shooting freely at the vermis rex. The worm didn't fall back from the bullets but did stop screaming. Instead of showing any signs of distress, it snapped at the five on the ground. Unable to see its aim was off. Its mouth jabbed at the wall next to them and then the ground just in front of the entrance. It was only a matter of time before it honed in on them.

"Our guns aren't working," screamed Eddie.

How do we kill it? Julianna asked Pip.

Their skin is incredibly difficult to penetrate. They are vicious and most haven't survived an encounter with them. Currently not finding anything of use.

Great. Well, currently, I'm smelling worm breath.

It was true. The giant worm seemed to be trying to suck in the room, taking in breaths. A mist of gross worm saliva sprayed down on all of them. The group had backed up several paces, and although the worm couldn't fit through the tunnel opening, with another force it could knock its way through.

"Thoughts?" asked Eddie.

"This tunnel we're in leads to a dead end. And the monster has a tough exterior that our guns won't work on, according to Pip," said Julianna.

"We can try explosives," said Fletcher, holding up the pack he'd been carrying.

The worm had started banging head first into the opening of the tunnel. This was the beginning of the end unless they acted fast.

Eddie pulled one of the blue marble grenades from his pocket. "Last one," he said, unscrewing it and launching it into the mouth of the worm.

There was a pause. The worm rose high into the air, like before. There was an eerie silence as everyone waited to see what happened next.

A ripple jerked down the worm and it twisted radically in the air before throwing itself down, mouth opening wide. Eddie and Julianna both looked at each other, not knowing what to expect next. The worm appeared stunned.

"Well that was easy," said Eddie.

A gurgling sound reverberated from the open mouth of the worm. Ominous doom fell down on Julianna as she spied the internal muscles beyond the dozen rows of teeth moving in a wave. It looked like it was about to throw up. "Why the fuck did you have to jinx us by saying that?" she asked.

"Incoming!" yelled Fletcher.

Julianna sprinted for the back of the tunnel just as a blast of hot air flew from the worm's mouth. It pushed her to the ground. Before she could stumble upright again, another assault hit her, this one wet and full of slime. She slipped one way then the other, trying to figure out what had happened. She managed to push the greenish sludge out of her face to see the others had been hit too with something slimy that smelled putrid.

The vermis rex had momentarily recovered and was back in the upright position. However, it looked to be trying to pull the rest of its body up from the opening in the ground. No telling what it was capable of when it was free. They were definitely screwed if they stayed in the tunnel.

She quickly made her way over the slippery ground to the four men closer to the entrance. They were all covered in the slime.

Eddie looked over his rifle. "I wouldn't advise we fire our weapons."

"Ground forces are still fighting off pirates from the forest. Seems they are coming in steady streams," said Fletcher.

"Which means we're on our own down here," said Julianna.

"Guns don't work," said Fletcher, holding up the pack, "but we still have explosives."

"We don't have time to set those properly," said Julianna, watching from the corner of her eye as the worm wiggled to try and get the rest of its body out of the hole. They didn't have much longer.

"No, we don't have that kind of time. But if I can set up these explosives close to its base, before it frees itself then we have a good chance," said Fletcher.

"And how are you going to get close enough for that?"

asked Eddie, running a handkerchief over his face—which did little to clear the green slime away.

"Well, the asshole can't see, can he?" asked Fletcher.

"Asshole…good one," said Eddie with a chuckle. "And no, he appears to rely on vibrations."

"So you need a distraction?" asked Julianna.

Fletcher turned to her with a crooked smile. "Bingo."

"That means the commander and I need to do the cha cha in the open space, is that right?" asked Eddie.

"Do whatever it is that you like, just distract that motherfucker," said Fletcher. "My men and I can set the explosives in less than a minute."

"What about the blast? Couldn't that cave us in if you're not laying them properly?" asked Julianna.

"I think anything is possible. We stay here and get eaten or we take a chance," said Fletcher.

He was right. They couldn't stay in this tunnel much longer and there was no way they were getting to the far side without seriously inflicting some damage on the worm. "Okay, fine. We will go with this plan. I want everyone back in this tunnel when we detonate," said Julianna.

"Yes, Commander," said Fletcher, saluting.

Julianna looked at Eddie, who had slime dripping from one of his eyebrows. "Ready to dance?" she asked, nearly smiling from the absurdity of this all. She almost wished the pirates were back. No wonder those jerks had sawed through the crystals. They were trying not to wake the beast. Hindsight.

"Let's do this. I vote we go to the left. That gives Fletcher more space for laying the explosives," said Eddie.

That area of the cave room was much larger and would offer more options. They had limited time and only one set of explosives. One chance to kill this beast.

"Okay, sounds good. Let's get as far as we can and then take turns distracting the monster," said Julianna.

Eddie nodded, seeming to instantly understand what she meant.

"On the count of three," said Eddie, poised and ready to sprint. "One, two—"

Julianna took off. She could never really wait for those dumb countdowns. Not when there was a job to do. Taking the lead, she jumped around stalagmites and rocks. The surface was slick but she rode along the slopes the best she could, staying close to the ground.

The worm monster screamed once and twisted around to face the direction she was running, abandoning its attempts to get out of the dirt.

She halted as the worm monster lowered down, its mouth puckered and only two feet in front of her. She slid back until she was flush against the cave wall. The vermis rex moved in closer, making Julianna tilt her head to the side, straight against the wall. She could smell the shit eater and he was disgusting.

"Hey fucker!" yelled Eddie who was roughly fifteen feet away.

Julianna, knowing the worm sensed through vibrations, didn't even breathe. Pip had apparently taken an intuitive note and slowed her heart down enough that it barely registered.

"Hey, you ugly son of a bitch! Want someone to vomit

on? Give it to me!" yelled Eddie, stomping his feet to get the monster's attention.

Julianna wanted to smile, but the whole fear-of-being-eaten-by-a-giant-worm thing prevented that.

The worm swiveled with an impressive grace until it was just in front of Eddie. He froze the same as Julianna. She could just make out Fletcher and his team sneaking out of the tunnel and around the worm. The monster jerked in their direction. Fuck. It was onto them.

Julianna kneeled, finding a few loose rocks. She rose up as steadily as she could and threw the stones towards the entrance where they'd come from. The vermis rex spiraled in that direction, menacingly surveying that area.

Fletcher and his men looked to be working quickly. Too quickly. The worm shot around, its mouth facing at its body, staring straight at the three men. They froze, all hunched over, laying explosives.

"Fuck face!" yelled Eddie. He picked up a large stalagmite that the worm had broken in its rage. He lifted it above his head and chucked it in the direction of its body farthest from Fletcher.

Like a dog easily distracted by a bone, the vermis rex curved, arching high in the air above Eddie. Its mouth opened showing the dozens of rows of razor sharp teeth. The scream took over Julianna's hearing, but she caught the visual of Fletcher and his men darting back to the tunnel. It was set.

Julianna darted for a crate of crystals sitting next to the wall. It was only half full, but hopefully that wouldn't matter. She launched the crate at the midsection of the worm. It rose high, screaming like it was offended by this crime. She threw herself into Eddie, barreling him in the direction of the tunnel. He sped up, carrying her as she carried him. They dove for the entrance, just making it inside as Fletcher detonated the explosive.

Julianna clapped her hands to her ears, her teeth biting hard together. Her skull rattled. The light blanketed her vision. She felt Eddie pull her closer, away from the blast. His arm covered her head from the explosion of debris and dust that whisked across the space.

A moment later and her lungs were overwhelmed. She began coughing from the smoke, the same as the others in the tunnel. The screaming had stopped, replaced by coughing and intense rattling all around them.

Julianna looked up, expecting to see the vermis rex lying in bits on the cave ground. It wasn't. Instead it was frozen in the same position it had been in before, arching overhead, mouth open. It swiveled until it was hanging just over the mouth of the tunnel.

"Fuck!" yelled Julianna.

"How did that not work?" asked Eddie, shuffling backwards on the ground, carrying Julianna with him as he did.

The rattling increased, making the ground, walls and ceiling shake.

The worm was really pissed now. They were out of options. Julianna kicked backwards as the vermis rex rammed hard into the tunnel, making debris rain down on them. Eddie kept his body perched slightly over hers.

Again the worm rammed hard into the cave, making everything rattle with more ferocity.

It paused seeming to study the vibrations. A hiss escaped it, blanketing them in hot air.

"Fuck my life," said Julianna, covering her mouth from the repugnant smell.

Then the vermis rex twisted around to the far wall, like hearing something. Was the team about to rescue them? The monster spun up and seemed to look straight at the crystal lined ceiling. A rattling so great it felt like they were on a trampoline rocked the cave. A chiming sound filled the air. Julianna had trouble figuring out where it came from until she looked up and saw the crystals swaying. *Swaying? How was that possible?*

The crystals overhead began to rock back and forth at odd angles and then they fell one by one. Bam! Over and over and over again they fell, shattering on the cave floor. Splinters of crystals sprinkled into the tunnel making the five retreat farther.

Still from their vantage point, Julianna noticed the worm panic. It looked to be trying to retreat back down the hole in which it had come from. However, it was stuck. That was evident. The crystals fell faster, like a hellacious hail storm.

Scream after scream ripped from the worm. It was no longer trying to escape, but rather was lying flat to the cave ground being pummeled repeatedly by sharp crystals. Each time one fell and pierced its tough skin the beast gave a convulsive jolt.

The crystals! Of course, thought Julianna.

Then all at once a cacophony of crystals fell, raining down in the cave room. Julianna covered her face from the splatter of glass and dust, trying as best she could to protect herself.

Are you alive? asked Pip in her head.

I think so, she answered.

What happened?

Can I give you a play-by-play if and when I get out of here?

Sure thing. We've handled the pirates. Looks like it is all clear.

Cool. I'll be out of here when I'm out of here.

Women. We always have to wait for you, said Pip, relief palpable in his voice despite his playfulness.

Julianna raised her head to find the worm punctured several times and lying limp in the middle of the cave room. Green blood oozed from the puncture wounds. Overhead the ceiling looked to be absent of many of the crystals. Instead their remnants were like shards of glass strewn across the ground.

Julianna stood, feeling like her legs needed a moment to adjust. She turned to Fletcher. "Still have that pack for the explosives?" she asked.

He blinked, orienting himself as well. "Yeah," he said, pulling the pack from his back.

"Good," said Julianna. "Have your men fill that and anything else you have with crystals and shards. I'm guessing the crates were destroyed. Let's take what we can. We're getting the fuck out of here."

Julianna turned to find Eddie staring around in disbelief. He had specks of blood on his face where the crystals had punctured his skin. "You all right, Edward?" she asked.

He blinked at her, looking a bit confused.

"What? Is everything all right?" she asked, worried he'd been hurt in a place she couldn't see.

"I'm fine," he said, shaking his head. "You called me 'Edward.'"

"Oh." Julianna blanched. "Right. You ready to head out?"

He surveyed the destroyed cave room with awe. "Yeah, I think we left our mark here. Let's fill up and get the fuck off this planet."

Julianna let out a heavy breath. "Agreed."

Cargo Bay, QBS *ArchAngel*, Davida System

"What is this?" asked Hatch, his typical irritation in his voice.

"That," began Eddie, pointing at the mounds of crystals shards they'd unloaded, "is the aether. You are welcome."

"*That* is dust," complained Hatch.

The injured had already been transported to the sick bay. Thankfully only two of Fletcher's team were shot, but any amount of injured is too many. Julianna and Eddie had brought the crystals to Hatch straight away, both joking about how insulted he'd be by what they brought back.

"Maybe they'll be easier to work with in this form," said Julianna, trying to hide a grin. She couldn't help it. Not once had they ever charged off and brought back exactly what Hatch wanted or not destroyed something he'd created. It was becoming a practical joke at this point.

"Or maybe it's lost its power," said Hatch, puffing up his cheeks. "I've never worked with aether like this."

"We considered looking for another cave to harvest, but there was that whole fear-of-being-eaten-alive-by-a-*vermis-rex*" explained Eddie.

Hatch waved him off with one of his tentacles. "The worm kings have been extinct on Berosia for centuries."

Eddie pulled off his boot, laughing as he did. "Oh, is that right? Well, I guess we were hallucinating when we were slimed by the monster." From his boot a dollop of green slime slipped and fell to the ground.

Julianna had wanted to shower after returning, but knew it was more important to deliver the crystals straight away. Besides they were heavy as hell and Eddie and she were able to make quick work of the transport.

Hatch's mouth fell open. He looked at Knox who was standing dutifully next to him. "That's not…?"

Knox, looking like he was on a lost planet, simply shrugged.

"Teach, you better not be messing with me," said Hatch, looking back at the captain.

"Playing with you about *what*? Why do you think the crystals are in bits?" asked Eddie, setting down his boot and pulling off his white sock which was green with slime. He went to wring it out. It's exactly what Julianna had wanted to do to her hair for the last hour, but hadn't had a spare moment. The slime covered every strand, making her look like she'd elected to use the worst hair gel ever.

Hatch's eyes widened suddenly. "No!" he yelled and his tentacle shot across the space, grabbing the sock from Eddie.

"Uh…what's the deal, Doc?" asked Eddie, looking bemused.

"The *deal* is that you two are covered in one of the most valuable, and thought to be one of the rarest, substances in the entire known galaxy," said Hatch, stretching his tentacle over to the work station where he deposited the sock into a clear tray. He pulled his tentacle back and wagged it in Eddie's face. "Do. Not. Move."

"Uh...why? What are you going to do?" asked Eddie, looking uncomfortable.

Hatch shook his head. "*I'm* not going to do anything to you. My poor apprentice has that job." He looked at Knox, a bit of a guiltless smile on his face. "Sorry kid, but that's the perk of being the boss."

"Ummm...Hatch," Julianna began. "What's going on? This stuff the *vermis rex* slimed us with is valuable?"

"Incredibly so. I'm going to need to extract as much of it from your clothes and bodies as possible," said Hatch, his voice growing with excitement. "Even if I just get a small amount then it will still be extremely useful. And then just imagine when you go back and tranquilize the vermis rex."

"*Tranquilize?*" asked Eddie, giving Julianna a look that accurately said, "We're fucking screwed."

Hatch was too busy retrieving tools from his workstation to notice the look. He handed a scraper tool and vial to Knox, ushering him over to Eddie. "Naturally. I'll have to develop the tranquilizer so that it doesn't harm the creature." Hatch looked up, his eyes overflowing with excitement. "Just think, this is probably the last one in existence, and we know where it is. If we play this right we can have enough..." He trailed away, looking interrupted by a thought.

Slowly Hatch lifted his gaze to look at Eddie, all the excitement gone. "Wait, why are the crystals all broken?"

"See…the thing is…that we didn't know that *vermis rex* was an endangered species," said Eddie, his tone tense, like he was backtracking. Knox had the scrapper and vial and was carefully combing bits of the slime from Eddie's clothing, making the whole situation tenser.

Hatch thrust a vial and scraper at Julianna, not daring to look at her. She took it and began trying to collect the disgusting slime. "*Extinct* species, actually, or so we thought. What did you do?"

"We really didn't have a choice," said Julianna. "I don't think we'd have made a different decision even if we had known it was supposedly extinct."

Hatch seemed to be wrestling with keeping his patience in check. "What did you do?"

"We tried to blow it up," confessed Eddie.

Hatch's face brightened. "That's not as bad as I thought."

"It's not?" asked Eddie, holding out his arm for Knox, trying to make his job easier.

"No. I mean, you probably destroyed the last *vermis rex* alive, but even blown up, we can still harvest its blood," said Hatch, a new light in his voice.

"Thing is that exploding it didn't work," explained Eddie.

"It didn't?" asked Hatch, his tone shifting. "Why not?"

"The outer skin is incredibly tough," said Eddie.

"Yes, the only thing that can penetrate it is the aether crystal…" Hatch trailed away, disappointment covering his face. He looked at Julianna. "How did you kill the *vermis rex*?"

"The explosion triggered a rainstorm of crystals," said Julianna, motioning to the crates of shards.

Hatch threw his tentacle to his head. "Of course you did!"

"We can still go back and harvest the disgusting monster," said Eddie quickly, trying to make amends for their blunder. "I'll even face down pirates again if it's that important."

"It would be worth you facing down all pirates in the galaxy, Teach," said Hatch. "But the only thing that neutralizes the *vermis rex*'s blood, rendering its properties useless is the aether crystal."

"Oops," said Eddie, looking down with shame.

Julianna tried extra hard to remove the slime, a sudden thought occurring to her. "This slime isn't dangerous, right? The lieutenant and a couple of his team members are covered in it too."

Hatch shook his head. "ArchAngel would you—"

"I'm already redirecting the men to you," said ArchAngel overhead. "I think you'll find that I'm—"

"Interrupting," said Hatch, angrily. "And no, Julie, it's not dangerous to you. Its properties when synthesized are incredible, but not in its purest form."

"What can it do?" asked Julianna, intrigued. Who would have thought the disgusting goo the monster spit on them would be so useful.

"Well, simply put, it can save a life. It's a cure for almost all infections, diseases and viruses," said Hatch, eyeing the vial she held up. It wasn't even half full. "However, I'm not sure we'll have enough for even a single dose."

"We'll do our best to extract as much as we can," said

Julianna, squeezing her hair into the vial, getting only a drop of slime. It had mostly been absorbed by her strands.

"Yeah, yeah," said Hatch shuffling off, his shoulders slumped. He turned, a new skepticism on his face. "And where, by the way, is my drone?"

Before Julianna could reply, Eddie chirped. "Jules lost it."

Intelligence Center, QBS *ArchAngel*, Behemoth System

Chester had kicked into high gear, trying to locate *Unsurpassed*. Searching for a ship inside of several systems was no easy feat...for most. He couldn't find just any ship, but since they had the blueprints from Deacon Flick for *Unsurpassed*, he knew one crucial detail. The ship had a trackable navigation system for those who knew where to look. If Felix had an AI supervising the ship then his hack would be detected, but the likelihood of that was close to zero. Felix may be smart and supplied with great technology, but having an AI was rare, especially for someone cast outside of the Federation.

"Are you coming?" Marilla asked from the doorway.

Chester hesitated once before hitting a single button. That single button tethered them to the *Unsurpassed* navigation system. It might take up to seventy-two hours to lock down a direction on it, but once it did then they'd know exactly where the ship was presently located. The reason for his hesitation was that the tracker came at a price. He'd know exactly where *Unsurpassed* was and until the system was disconnected, *Unsurpassed* could find out exactly where QBS *ArchAngel* was located. That was only a concern if they were detected, though.

Chester let out a heavy breath and plastered a smile on his face. He spun to face Marilla, popping up from his seat. "Yeah, I'm totally ready. Let's go kick some butt," he said, striding over to her.

She had a worried look on her face. Truthfully Marilla often looked a little worried, like she was always pondering some of life's more serious questions. She probably was. However, presently, she looked more concerned about something immediate based on the weight in her eyes.

"Everything all right?" asked Chester, walking beside her, Harley taking the lead.

She wheeled around, halting just in front of him. "You're crazy to do this. You're not a soldier and aren't trained for this sort of thing."

Chester didn't need to ask her about what she was referring to. They'd been skirting this topic all week. And here it was finally, out in the open.

"I know. You're totally right," said Chester, unable to suppress a proud smile. "I'm probably going to die."

"Don't say that," said Marilla, her voice full of real fear.

"It's true. I'm sneaking onto an enemy ship and hacking into their database. If they catch me then I'll be the first one they slaughter," said Chester, enjoying this too much.

"Then you shouldn't go. We both know it," said Marilla.

"No, we both know that I *have* to go. What do you think

I'm going to do? Give the captain a crash course on graduate level hacking real quick?"

"You could direct him remotely. You've done it before," urged Marilla.

Chester shook his head. "This is much too complicated for something like that. I've thought this through. I need to be on that ship."

"There has to be another way though," said Marilla.

Chester pulled off his glasses, cleaning them with the hem of his shirt. "You know, Mar, I've been hunted by deadly pirates. They've chased me across a dozen planets. I appreciate your concern, but I'm not a wimp."

Marilla looked like the breath had just been sucked from her. "I didn't say you were. I just…"

"Don't want me to die," said Chester, completing her sentence. "That isn't love, but it definitely reeks of your concern for my wellbeing. I'll take it."

"Love?" Marilla asked, back up suddenly. "Who said anything about love?"

Chester smiled, putting back on his glasses. "I believe you did, dear Mar." He strode off, leaving her gaping at his back.

Cargo Bay, QBS *ArchAngel*, Behemoth System

"Don't tell the captain, but this form of the crystals makes this all easier," said Hatch, grunting as he worked on the cloaking belt.

Knox looked up from the project he'd been assigned. "Why should we keep that from the captain?"

"No reason," said Hatch quickly. Knox was trying so

hard to impress him that he hadn't really loosened up yet and realized that part of the job was ripping into your team. Well, that was part of the fun for Hatch anyway. Everyone had their thing.

"Doctor A'Din Hatcherik would never want the captain to know he hadn't messed up thoroughly," supplied Pip overhead.

Hatch looked up, his eyes narrowing. "Why have the AIs on this ship increasingly decided to be a pain in my ass?"

"I think it would be impossible for us to actually do that, Doctor A'Din Hatcherik," said Pip, sounding amused.

"Fine, let me rephrase. Why do you two keep irritating the hell out of me?" asked Hatch.

"We are only offering our supreme intelligence and insight," chimed in ArchAngel.

Hatch turned away from the cloaking belt he was working on. He only had one right now, although they needed three and pronto. However, he wasn't yet comfortable enough with Knox to work in the style that he was used to: with every tentacle acting seamlessly in unison, performing the tasks of half-a-dozen men. He knew it was an alarming sight and didn't care to share something so personal. He wouldn't stand to have his apprentice view him as a freak.

"We also supply great entertainment," said Pip.

"If you're referring to your knock-knock jokes, then don't include me," said ArchAngel.

"You know, ArchAngel is kind of a mouthful to say," said Pip, mischief in his voice. "Can we rename you?"

"No," answered ArchAngel at once.

"What do you want to rename her?" asked Hatch, intrigued by any idea that would irritate the AI. It wasn't that he really liked antagonizing as that he loved that he had two AIs he could banter with. He'd never tell anyone this, but working with Ghost Squadron was a dream come true at a time in his career when he'd thought he'd forever be stagnant. He worked on the ArchAngel. He had a sample of vermis rex blood. And enough aether crystals to cloak a planet, if he wanted to. Life was good. And it just kept getting better.

"I'm not going to be renamed. The Queen herself named—"

"I found a record of a device on Earth that humans had in their homes which is similar to what we do," began Pip. "Although not sentient, the computers were meant to assist the humans in day-to-day tasks, making their homes smarter and their lives easier. The device was given a name that would be the least likely to be said by accident so it wouldn't get confused with other words."

"There are no issues with my current name," insisted ArchAngel, sounding increasingly more irritated by the moment.

Hatch snickered to himself, working as he did.

"No, sure there isn't," said Pip. "Aren't-cha able to sleep?"

"I know what you're trying to do," said ArchAngel dryly, not impressed.

"We think the problem comes down to arch...aeolgy," said Pip, taking a beat before adding the last bit.

"Do I need to remind you how simplistic the name Pip is?" asked ArchAngel.

"Go ahead and remind me," spat Pip. "Tell me all about how my name can be confused with pipes and piper… Oh, wait, it can't. Different phonetic."

"I can disable you from *ArchAngel*, making it so you can't interface with others," threatened ArchAngel.

Knox burst out laughing, catching Hatch by surprise. "If she's making threats then I think you're getting to her."

"Knox Gunnerson, you should stay out of this," said ArchAngel.

"Don't let her intimidate you, Gunner," said Pip. "Now, my research shows that having a soft syllable followed by an *x* is the best combination to avoid confusion. However, we don't even need to do any testing. Instead we can rename you after the little devices that were in modern homes on Earth."

"I refuse to be renamed," said ArchAngel.

"What was the name?" asked Knox, looking pleasantly amused. Working with Ghost Squadron had to be a dream come true for him. It was interesting to Hatch that he and his apprentice could come from two different walks of life and find their dream job in the same place.

"Alexa!" chirped Pip, excitedly.

"This conversation is over," said ArchAngel.

"Oh, okay," said Pip. "Goodbye Alexa."

"Grrr…" came her voice before she went silent.

Recreation Hall, QBS *ArchAngel*, Behemoth System

Cheers erupted from the crowd as Julianna's bowling ball knocked over all the pins. It was her sixth consecutive strike.

"You really make this look easy," said Eddie, standing to take his turn just as Chester and Marilla joined the group.

"There isn't anything to it," said Julianna. "Unlike with most sports, if you get the initial move down then you don't have to do anything else."

"You mean, master the strike and then you never have to learn any other skill?" asked Fletcher, sitting across from her.

"Yes, something like that. The problem comes when only a few of the pins go down," explained Julianna.

"So I guess you've figured out the way to always get a strike," said Fletcher.

"Given that all factors are the same, then yes. Weight of the ball, surface of the lane and air density does factor in from time to time," said Julianna.

"But you have Pip to account for each of these and advise," said Chester, grabbing a ball from the rack and adding it with the rest.

"Usually I would, but he informed me earlier he was going to go and harass someone named Alexa," said Julianna.

Eddie threw his bowling ball. It sped down the lane at lightning speed and then popped over to the gutter and then to the neighboring lane where it knocked down all the pins.

He turned, expecting to receive cheers. Lars, who was about to take his turn in the nearby lane and was staring at no pins, frowned. "I don't think I can count that for me," he said, pretending to be offended.

"Teach, you're supposed to knock down *your* pins," joked Julianna. "Not ones in other lanes."

"Oops, sorry Lars," said Eddie. "I'm still getting used to my strength." He strolled back just as Marilla took a seat. She looked pretty sullen, which concerned him since the girl was usually quite pleasant. As typical, she didn't join the activity but instead had brought a book. Marilla was always reading, but he respected that she still joined the team building activities. He thought they were important for bonding and morale. Julianna told him she thought it was just his opportunity to show off. That was probably true, although she was the one showing off today.

Fletcher lined up with his ball. He, as Jack had advised, had been a seamless addition to Ghost Squadron. His team, which were dispersed around the other neighboring lanes, playing as well, had been instrumental already. It was strange how fast Ghost Squadron was growing and pressed the significance of what they were doing into Eddie. More than ever before, he was doing something that truly mattered. There was a weight that went along with that, but he hadn't quite felt it. Maybe when the newness of his enhanced body wore off, although Julianna said that never really happened.

Fletcher threw his ball and Harley sprang out from underneath Marilla's seat, racing down the lane after it. There was a split second where the dog must have realized he'd entered a slick territory. His legs slipped out from underneath him and he dove chest first on the lane, gliding down after the ball.

Marilla shot into a standing position. "Harley!"

Eddie sprinted forward, running down the area between the gutters after the dog. He was already trying to push up, but the overly oiled floor made it nearly impossible to stand.

Reaching down, Eddie pulled the dog from the lane, carrying him down the walkway. "Someone is going to be pissed at you for messing up the lanes," he whispered to the dog.

The crowd cheered when Harley was set back down on the floor. He ran under the chairs, looking embarrassed.

Eddie took his seat next to Julianna, a smile on his face.

"Dumb dog," said Julianna. "You should have left him there."

"You don't mean that," said Eddie.

She looked at him, trying her best to appear serious. Still, under the tough expression he saw something, something she was hiding. "Don't I?" she asked, challenging him.

"No, I know you. Despite your restraint, you like that dog," said Eddie.

"I'm not sure why it would matter," said Julianna, indifferently.

"Because if you can warm up to a 'mangy dog' as you like to call him, then anything is possible," said Eddie, giving her a soft smile. "I have high hopes for you, Jules."

"Don't waste your time with such hopes," she said, standing to take her turn.

16

Alpha-line Q-Ship, Airspace outside *Unsurpassed*, Tangki System

"I still can't believe you bowled a perfect game," remarked Chester, securing his helmet over his head. His voice switched to coming through the comm.

"You would if you'd seen me do it the dozen times before," said Julianna. "If we're ever at a bar with bowling or shuffle board, don't tell anyone my secret. It's one of my many ways of taking stranger's cash."

Eddie's smile could be seen through the front plate of his own helmet. "How'd I get paired up with two sharks for this mission? One at pool and the other at bowling," he said proudly.

From the cockpit, Lar's voice rang out. "We're nearly in position."

Julianna looked out the side panel of the air lock where they stood, all of them suited up for space travel. They stood in a secure chamber, partitioned off from the main cabin. Chester had found *Unsurpassed*, using a tracker. He'd also been able to determine an airlock where they could enter through. It would get the attention of someone on the bridge, but that's why Eddie and Julianna were there.

Eddie checked that the tether between the three of them was tight. He was in the lead. Chester in between them.

"We're all set," said Eddie to Lars. "Opening the air lock in the back chamber in ten seconds."

"Copy," said Lars.

"Initiate cloaking belts," said Julianna, opening her own and activating. A moment later and the three disappeared from the space.

"That's wild," said Chester. She appreciated having him on this mission. He was fearless and appreciated the thrill of the adventure. Most might be worried about taking a computer hacker on a mission like this, but she knew since the moment they met Chester Wilkerson that he was a force to be feared both on the Dark Web and in person. It was because of him that she'd been shot at and electrocuted, all because of his cleverly built traps. This was not a guy to be underestimated.

Eddie led the way across the short expanse between the cloaked Q-Ship and *Unsurpassed*. Now that he was floating next to the enemy ship, he could see how incredibly it was built. Although not as big as QBS *ArchAngel*, it still was a size to impress. He could only wonder about the thing Felix could be plotting with a ship this big. Was it a war? A direct attack on the Federation? He definitely had a ship that could put up quite the fight, especially since it had the same shielding technology as the smaller ship he'd used when they'd last met him.

Opening the airlock from the outside would have posed a problem before. However, with a device that Hatch had equipped them with and his super human skill, it was as easy as pie. Eddie had never made a pie before, actually. He remembered that his mother said the crust was the hardest part. He smiled to himself, thinking of his mother. *This is for you, Mom. All of this has always been for you and Dad.*

Eddie felt the tug as Chester's cord lost its slack. He pulled on it, dragging the hacker into the safe chamber between the main ship and the air lock. When the door to the air lock closed, he let out a giant breath. *So far, so good.*

"Okay, we're about to have company," said Eddie over the comm.

He opened the next vault door, quickly making his way to the other side. He heard footsteps down the corridor ahead, now that his suit had been switched over to pick up outside noises.

"Leave the baddies to us, Chester." said Eddie. "Go do what we came here for."

"I'm on it," said Chester over the comm.

"And stay cloaked and on the radio. Let us know if you run into trouble," said Julianna. "Otherwise, we'll be here, waiting for you to return."

"Copy, Commander," said Chester.

Just then three armed guards appeared, staring at the airlock chamber in confusion. Their system would have told them it had been opened. Their eyes were telling them that it was in fact closed and the area around it deserted.

"I'll take the one of the left. You take the one on the right," said Eddie.

"Your left or mine?" asked Julianna.

"Good point," said Eddie. "I've got this one."

He waited until the first guard was a little closer and then grabbed both of his shoulders and yanked him down hard, throwing his knee into the guy's abdomen.

"Okay. Gotcha," said Julianna, going after the next guard, who was shocked by what was invisibly attacking the first.

Eddie flipped his guard around easily, pulling restraints from his belt and securing them around his hands.

"What about the third?" asked Julianna, making quick work of her guard. His face was already pressed down to the floor, a pinched expression on his face.

"Well, I was hoping we were going to fight over him, but damn the fucker!" The third guard had changed direction, running back the way he came. Eddie bounded after him.

"Don't let him get away," said Julianna. "We don't need the attention."

"Not to worry," said Eddie, easily talking as he sped after the guard. He was only a few feet away when he dove, grabbing around his waist and wrestling him to the ground.

"Please, no. Please," cried the guard.

Eddie wished he could tell the guy it was just going to hurt a little. However, it was best if he didn't. The guy continued to sob and then screamed out loudly. With no other option, Eddie flipped the guy over and slugged him once in the face. The guards face flew to the side and he passed out immediately.

"This one is going to need a gag," said Eddie, standing and dragging the body back to where the others were.

Unsurpassed, **Tangki System**

Just breeze down the corridor and stroll onto the bridge. No biggie, thought Chester. He was invisible anyway. That had always been the super hero skill he wanted growing up, over flying and enhanced strength. The invisible person had all the advantages. Well, unless they aroused suspicion and made too much noise. But he wouldn't be so careless.

You're good, he told himself. Just find an unused work station and a minute, maybe two later and, he'd be all done. Really, he could access the main network for *Unsurpassed* from any computer aboard. However, from the bridge there would be fewer obstacles. Those computers were usually connected straight to the main frame.

A group of uniformed men strode out of a nearby room, striding shoulder to shoulder. *Fuck!* Why did people have to walk side by side? *Single file, bitches*, thought Chester. He didn't know how he would get past them. He was invisible, but still could be felt. He still made noise and affected his environment.

A door ahead of him was the only thing between him and the uniforms who were talking jovial. Chester made an impromptu decision and slapped the button for the door, making it retract. He jumped into the empty room and slid up against the wall inside.

One of the uniformed individuals peeped in. "Why do you think the door opened?" he asked his companion.

"Who knows. Maybe a glitch. The lieutenant said there looked to be something out of the ordinary going on with one of the air locks," said the other guard. "Come on. I'm starving. Let's grab some grub before it's gone."

The other guard didn't budge, instead looked around the room. He turned and looked straight at Chester. The guy had no idea he was looking straight at the intruder. Hopefully, he'd never learn that there was one.

Finally, the guy shrugged. "Yeah, I guess you're right."

He retreated granting Chester a moment to finally breathe.

"What was that about, Chester?" asked Eddie over the comm.

He waited an extra second before saying, "It's all good. I just had to give a couple guards the slip."

"Okay, well, we've got about five minutes before they send someone to check on these deployed guards," said Eddie.

"So get on it," said Chester. "Yeah, I'm on my way.

Chester ran, not even giving much concern for the sounds his footsteps made. The hallway was empty. However, ahead, on the bridge he could hear different voices and pings and beeps as equipment was used and reports monitored. The bridge was always a busy place on a ship and therefore the perfect place for a trespassing. *Hide in plain sight, right?*

The next main room, as he knew from the plans, was the bridge. It was large with a dozen work stations. Chester peeled around the first two where communication officers were working, doing whatever they did. He took a seat at a workstation behind them that sat alone from the rest. It was perfect.

Chester was into the main system after only a few attempts. He slammed his finger triumphantly down on the "Enter" key. This earned a curious backward glance from one of the officers in front of him. Even though he was cloaked, he shrunk down. If they chanced a glance at his screen right then they'd see something that would flag suspicions.

After a moment the officer turned around, being redirected by the commander of the ship.

Felix Castile. The evil mastermind himself stood in the center of the bridge, hands clasped behind his back and gaze on the glowing map screen before him. The man had narrowed eyes and a pointy chin.

"What sort of malfunctions could be happening with the airlocks?" asked Felix.

A squatty man with a round face leaned over and whispered in his ear. Chester shook off the distraction, refocusing on the task at hand.

He slipped a drive into the slot on the side of the workstation. It lit up green, making his heart skip. If someone saw this it would give him away immediately. He thought about getting caught. Tortured. He'd acted tough when Marilla was worried, but truthfully all Chester had ever done was flee when the situation warranted. He'd never snuck onto a ship and stole covert information.

The system opened up easily, like a first flower of spring, eagerly hungry for light. *Perfect. Now just twenty more seconds.* It helped that Chester knew exactly what he was looking for. Well, and he was damn brilliant.

This was going to go off without a hitch. He'd have the data and be back in the airlock in under a minute. He couldn't wait to relay the information to the captain and the commander.

"What do you mean?" asked Felix, his voice rising.

"Sir, we've found a tracking intruder. It was hooked onto our navigation," said one of his officers to him.

Oh no! Fuck fuck fuck! Chester glanced at his screen. Ten more seconds.

"What ship is tracking us?" asked Felix, his voice flaring with anger.

"It's the *ArchAngel*," said the officer.

"Disconnect from them," ordered Felix.

"We're trying, sir, but our initial attempts failed," said the officer.

He spun around and bared down on the squatty officer. "Does this have to do with the airlock?"

"I-I-I don't know," said the officer.

"Well, find out," Felix bellowed.

"Sir?" asked the officer.

Ping. The drive download was complete. Chester yanked it out of the workstation, and unconcerned for noise he bolted out of the bridge. He sprinted.

"We learned that we also have the location for the Arch-Angel, because of the tracker," said the officer to Felix.

"Fuck! Fuck! Fuck!" said Chester, this time loud enough for Eddie and Julianna to hear over the comm.

"What is it? Are they headed this way?" asked Julianna.

"I don't know. Probably," said Chester, breathless. Fuck, he couldn't easily get to his inhaler in his pocket because of the suit nor did he have time to spare. "I'm headed this way, but more importantly is that they know we tracked them."

Chester rounded the corner. One long hallway separated him from the airlock, from his escape.

"So they know we're aboard?" asked Eddie.

"That's not the biggest problem. They know where *ArchAngel* is," said Chester.

"Fuck! What do we do?" asked Julianna.

"I need to get back on the ship. That's the only way to disconnect the program," said Chester, heaving.

"Can't ArchAngel do it?" asked Eddie.

"If she knows my forty-eight digit code," said Chester, arriving just in front of Eddie and Julianna.

"No time for that," said Eddie, pulling open the chamber door. "We've got to get out of here. *ArchAngel* will be fine for a moment. She's tough."

The three arrived on the Q-Ship with a bit of a surprise. The blast knocked them back before they had a chance to secure the airlock all of the way. Julianna held onto Eddie, pulling him back as he grabbed the hatch.

"Cloak the ship!" yelled Julianna to Lars. He had to take the cloak off for a moment so they could find their way to the ship. With *Unsurpassed* on high alert, they were fast to fire on the ship.

Julianna and Eddie slammed into the far wall when the ship sped off. The good news was they were cloaked and there was no tracking on the ship. The bad news was that it didn't matter if QBS *ArchAngel* was cloaked. The ship's position was being broadcast to *Unsurpassed.*

"Pip, update ArchAngel on the situation. Put her on red alert and get her ready to gate," said Eddie.

"She's been informed," said Pip. "She wants to gate and meet us at specified coordinates."

"No!" yelled Chester. He pulled his helmet off, his breathing labored. "If *ArchAngel* gates now, then *Unsurpassed* will just follow her. I need to get aboard that ship and disable it. It's the fastest way. If the code isn't put in correctly, then it has a failsafe and will block all other attempts for up to an hour."

"Damn, you failsafed your failsafe?" asked Eddie.

"I was tracking an enemy's navigation," explained Chester. "I had to make it so that if they tried to disconnect they'd hit a huge wall. Otherwise we probably wouldn't have located them."

"Tell me you made all this worth it," said Julianna, scanning Chester.

He reached out his hand and laid a disk drive in her hand. "Give this to the general. It will tell him exactly what Felix is planning."

"We're coming in for a landing," said Lars overhead. "Brace yourself. This is going to be a rough one."

"What about you?" asked Eddie, looking at Chester who had his eyes wide as he grabbed onto the cargo hold for support.

"I'm going to run like hell to the Intelligence Center," said Chester. "I'll let you know once we're disconnected. Then we jump."

The Q-Ship landed hard on the port side, knocking them all to the side. It sputtered back and forth, rotating to the starboard side before it hit a wall in the landing bay. Julianna bumped her head hard into the side of the ship. Chester was about to do the same, but she shot forward and put her body between his and the wall. He knocked into her, but she took the brunt of the impact. When the ship slowed, she pushed him up and off her. He was breathing hard, his chest making a wheezing sound.

"You okay?" she asked.

"Yes, I'll be fine," said Chester as the hatch opened. "Now, I've got to fix this."

And he was gone, running like she'd never seen him.

17

QBS *ArchAngel*, Tangki System

Chester barreled down the corridor, his feet nearly flying out from underneath him as he made his way to the Intelligence Center. His lungs ached and his breath felt too short. He didn't dare stop, though, to retrieve the inhaler he kept in his pockets for just such an occasion. There wasn't any time.

Chester pushed past confused crew members as he sprinted through the hallway. Many clogged the corridor, making him have to yell.

"Coming through. Emergency. Move! Move! Move!" yelled Chester, his face red and hot. They no doubt wondered why he was wearing a space suit and pushing everyone back as he ran.

Fuck! Chester thought, whizzing around a bend.

Something jolted the ship, knocking him hard into the nearest wall. His nose made first contact making him think he'd broken it. Chester pushed away, continuing to run.

His eyes watering and a pinching sensation made it harder to breathe.

Overhead, red lights began to strobe as a low siren started. It wasn't obtrusive, but accurately communicated the message: we're under attack.

Chester grabbed the doorway, rounding into the Intelligence Center.

"Chester!" yelled Marilla, surprised. He didn't even take a second to look at her, but instead sped for his seat, flinging it out of the way.

"Not now!" yelled Chester, typing in his password immediately.

The computer flashed. "Invalid password."

Damn it, why did he have to make his passwords so complicated? He tried to take in a steady breath. He couldn't do *this* unless he kept his cool. However, the breath was more of a wheeze.

"You're having an asthma attack," said Marilla, breaking into his thoughts.

Yes, it was true. He leaned forward, putting his head between his knees, trying to calm is diaphragm.

Marilla pushed into his shoulder. She was rummaging in his desk, but he couldn't concentrate on anything but his failed attempts to breathe. His head swam with dizziness. Soon he'd pass out and then they'd all be screwed.

"Here," said Marilla, her tone at high alert. She pulled him up and thrust the inhaler into his hand. The one he kept in his desk at the bottom drawer. With the stress weighing on him, he'd forgotten about that.

"Thank—" he tried to say, but couldn't get out the word. Instead, he stuck the inhaler to his mouth and took three puffs. It was more than his usual dose, but this was worse than his usual attack.

His vision started to return to normal, but he still felt dizzy.

The ground under them shook. The walls of the ship rattled.

Marilla stabilized herself by holding onto his desk. Chester fell forward on the keyboard. He dropped to his knees when the next blast hit.

"ArchAngel," said Chester, typing each key with precision as the ship shook under him. He couldn't make another mistake or his system would lock him out. Then they'd be screwed. Really screwed.

"Yes, Chester," said ArchAngel.

"I'm disconnecting the tracker. At my command you will be cleared to jump the ship," said Chester.

"How long will that take?" asked ArchAngel.

Chester hit two more keys, trying to steady himself. "Hopefully just another few minutes."

"Defenses are up, but we're taking hits. Do we have time to send out Black Eagles?" asked ArchAngel.

"No! Just…give…me…a…minute," said Chester, typing his password out carefully with each letter.

His screen shifted, allowing him into his system.

"Perfect," he rejoiced.

His fingers moved furiously, navigating to the right window. All he had to do was input the passcode and disconnect the tracker.

Another hit nearly made Chester's legs fly out from under him. *Just one more minute,* he thought, tapping hard on his desk, waiting for the system to update.

It was the longest minute of his life.

"This wing is the one under the most fire," said Arch-Angel. "Fire has broken out in the rafters below. I must advise that you vacate as soon as possible."

"I'm trying to keep us from being blown up," said Chester.

"*Unsurpassed* is hitting us with everything they have," said ArchAngel. "I can retaliate strongly, but it will deplete the energy reserves for the next jump."

"No, we have to jump," said Chester. *This was all his fault.* They'd been ambushed. *ArchAngel* wouldn't ever be in a situation like this otherwise. They could have made this a quick fight if positioned right. Yes, they could have taken Felix out when they first knew where *Unsurpassed* was located, but they'd also take out many innocent crew members. Chester knew that Eddie and Julianna would never go for that.

An explosion rocked him forward. It was in the corridor just outside.

"Chester!" yelled Marilla. "We have—"

"I can't!" yelled Chester, spinning around. "This is all my fault. I'm the only one who can fix it. Run, Marilla! Get out of here. I'm fine."

He spun around. There was only one thing left to do. Navigate to the tracker. Input passcode. And done. They'd be free and clear.

"I'm not leaving you," yelled Marilla. She inched in closer to Chester. "You can do this. Just remember to breathe."

For all the things that Marilla could have said right then, that was the most valuable. *Breathe, Chester,* he thought, realizing he'd been holding his breath. That was the last thing he should be doing right then, with his lungs already on fire. Chester drew in a few short breaths, followed by a giant one.

One last step. All he had to do was disconnect the tracker. He slapped the enter key. The system processed.

Across the screen, a single message popped up: *Tracking device terminated.*

Julianna and Eddie had divided up. He had agreed to go up to the bridge to oversee the defense operations. Julianna, at ArchAngel's direction, had sped down to the wing taking the most damage. She was in search of the hurt or stranded. Fights on ships could get out of hand pretty quickly and there was always a domino factor that made things exponentially worse.

"Chester has been successful," said ArchAngel overhead as Julianna sprinted down the corridor streaked with fire.

"Thank fucking goodness," said Julianna, trying not to breath too deeply and suffocate on the fumes.

"Gating will commence in five, four, three, two, and *one*," said ArchAngel.

Julianna paused, but only briefly enough to absorb the impact of the jump. It always threw her off balance, making her head feel like it exploded before being put back together again.

She inhaled a larger breath than she meant to and blinked the smoke out of her eyes.

"I need to close off this sector as soon as the last humans, Chester and Marilla, vacate," said ArchAngel.

"Where are they?" asked Julianna.

"They will be crossing your path in three, two and—"

Ahead through the smoke and fire, two figures emerged, hand-in-hand. Marilla pulled Chester as they ran.

"Good. There you two are," said Julianna, urging them to keep running. "Get to safety."

"Yes, Commander," yelled Chester, his voice a little weak. He was still wearing his suit, unlike Julianna who had thrown it off.

"ArchAngel," said Julianna. "You said Chester and Marilla were the last down here. We're clear to close off this wing now?"

"I said they were the last humans down here," said ArchAngel.

Julianna stopped. "What?"

"Harley, the canine, appears to have been frightened and run to the opposite side of this corridor. He's trapped in a back storage room due to an internal explosion," said ArchAngel.

"Fuck me" yelled Julianna. She turned back to watch Chester and Marilla retreating. Then she turned back to the corridor, ablaze with fire.

What are you thinking? asked Pip.

I'm thinking I've lost my mind.

You're not considering—

It's my ship, and I have to do what is expected of me. Julianna hesitated for one more second before sprinting into the fire after the dog.

The heat of the flames made Julianna's hairline sweat. She ignored it and crouched low, trying to slow her breathing. Smoke snaked its way through this corridor, getting thicker as she walked.

"Why did Harley have to go down here?" asked Julianna, trying not to part her mouth much to talk. This wing was mostly deserted, usually used for storage. The Intelligence Center was sparking, the fire had traveled up through the floor.

"Harley was scared and unknowingly ran in the wrong direction," said Archangel. "A simple enhancement would prevent this from happening in the future. It would provide a host of benefits."

An explosion, this one in the pipes running along the ceiling, rained down sparks and debris. Julianna covered her head, speeding up. "Let's just hope he survives long enough for such a thing," mumbled Julianna.

"The fire and smoke from this sector is close to infecting the neighboring ones," stated ArchAngel.

"I know, I know," said Julianna. "I need to find the dog first. Just give me another minute."

"Harley is straight ahead in the storage closet. It appears to have a rafter blocking the door," said ArchAngel.

"I was hoping this was going to be easy," said Julianna, nearly crawling. The smoke burned her eyes and made her vision blurry.

I've turned off your pain receptors, stated Pip.

Thanks, but my skin can still melt off even if I don't feel it.

Your heart can stop and you can suffocate, too. All I can do is prevent you from feeling your death.

That's a morbid thought as I cross into the fire zone.

Julianna took off at a sprint, hurdling over a line of fire. She landed in a safe place, but was encircled by flames.

"The temperature is rising at an alarming rate," stated ArchAngel.

"I'm aware. I think my boot is about to melt into the floor," said Julianna. She could see the closet. It was blocked by a fallen overhead beam. Fire licked at the wall from all sides, framing the storage unit. She was only heartened by the fact that the storage rooms were usually insulated due to the chemicals they held. Harley probably wasn't dead…yet…maybe…

"You should be aware that the captain is livid with you right now for taking this risk," said ArchAngel.

"Good. It's about time I returned the favor," said Julianna, shielding her face from the flames.

She was half grateful she'd slipped out of her space suit upon arriving back on the QBS *ArchAngel* because she could move faster. She was also wishing she still had the protection of the suit now. However, one of the other good parts was that she had her clothes to use. The flames and smoke were overwhelming. She pulled off her long sleeved under armor shirt, making her exposed, except for her sports bra.

Julianna ripped the shirt in half, tying one part of it around her nose and mouth, protecting her somewhat from the smoke. She wrapped the rest of the shirt around her hands. She may not be able to feel anything, but her hands could still be badly burned. That would slow her down and every second counted.

Reaching out, she sucked in a small breath as she tried to haul the beam off of the door. It was fucking jammed though.

"I'm not allowing the captain into this corridor, but I can't hold him back much longer and I need to shut down this section," said ArchAngel.

"So we're about to both be trapped in here, is that what you're saying?" asked Julianna, gritting her teeth as she tried again to unhinge the beam. It wouldn't budge.

"I'm saying that you need to get out of there. Your air quality is at a toxic level," said ArchAngel.

Julianna held back the urge to cough. "I'll be fine. I just…need…to…get… this…off!" Julianna fell back as the beam shot out of place. She trampled back into the fire but recovered quickly, slapping the fire off her arms and legs. Not wasting a moment, Julianna wrenched the door open.

There, crouched at the back of the storage unit, which was thankfully free from smoke and flames, stood Harley, looking smaller somehow.

"There you are!" Julianna exclaimed. She held out her hands to the cowering dog. His ears perked up and he bounded forward, seeming to understand the urgency for speed. Harley bounded forward, jumping straight into Julianna's arm. He was a large dog, but not so much so that he didn't fit in her arms. Julianna whipped around, racing through the obstacle course of fire and fallen overhead structures.

She ducked under a low beam that had fallen, making Harley yelp when his head glided too close to fire. "I'm doing the best I can, buddy," she said, trying to keep her breath steady.

"Oxygen levels are nearing less than sixteen percent," informed ArchAngel.

"And I'm almost out of here, so just keep it open one more minute," said Julianna, the dog bouncing in her arms as she ran. Ahead she could see the Intelligence Center which was now engulfed in flames.

"Need to proceed with extinguishing sequence now that you're returning," said ArchAngel.

"Which will what? Cover me in steam?" asked Julianna.

"Exactly. I wanted to wait until you found the dog or otherwise you would have been blinded by the smoke," said ArchAngel. "And also, I tried to avoid extinguishing, thinking we could close off the damaged areas."

"But it spread too quickly," said Julianna.

"Extinguishing mode commencing," said ArchAngel and overhead the sprinkler system fired on, raining fire suppression agents down on the flame, making steam spout up. Julianna's eyes watered more than ever, but she was grateful she couldn't feel the stinging.

She jumped over a smoking floor. Wires had fallen out of the ceiling and were sparking. Julianna sped up, seeing a figure in the distance. His arms were waving over him, but it was hard to make out his face, due to the steam which was cloaking everything.

There was a line of fire which was putting up a fight to the sprinklers. Julianna's boot nearly slipped out from under her when she sprinted forward and leapt over the fire. It grazed her legs and feet, but she made it over the flame, still clutching Harley.

Now she could see Eddie on the other side of the hatch entrance. He'd dutifully stayed back, but his face expressed his frustration about being detained. Julianna looked over her shoulder just as an explosion rocked the ship, launching her forward. She nearly tripped over her feet, but caught herself before falling on Harley. He flew out of her arms and landed on his feet. Then he ran on ahead of her, clearing the hatch and then bounding on in the direction of safety.

Julianna jumped over the partition for the door and kept running until she wasn't being sprinkled with water overhead. She turned when she heard the hatch door shut and lock.

"Section B has been closed off and is being decontaminated," stated ArchAngel.

Julianna yanked the remnants of her shirt off her face and wiped the sweat and chemicals from her forehead. She looked up to find Eddie staring at her with an expression she'd never seen before. He was angry, his eyes pinched and mouth in a flat line.

"What were you thinking?" he asked, letting out a giant exhale.

Julianna instantly felt cold. Pip must have reactivated her pain receptors. She shivered from the water. Crossing her arms in front of her chest, she suddenly remembered she was shirtless. She stared down a bit awkwardly and then shook it off, standing tall and proud.

"I only did exactly what you would have done in my situation," said Julianna.

Eddie's jaw worked back and forth like he was

measuring his resolve. Then he softened. Smiled. Relaxed. "Yeah, I guess you did."

"You're just mad that I beat you to the rescue," said Julianna.

Eddie's smile dropped as he looked down the long corridor in the direction where Harley had run. "I'm just glad you're alright and that I was right."

"Right? Right about what?" asked Julianna.

"I knew you had a soft spot for Harley."

"I guess I do like the scraggly dog, against my better instincts," admitted Julianna.

"Good thing, too, because I consider myself to be a mutt of sorts," said Eddie. He strode forward and wrapped his arm around her shoulder, leading her off.

18

QBS *ArchAngel*, Tangki System

Eddie watched as the general's eyes scanned back and forth over the report. Finally, after a long stretch of silence, punctuated only by Jack nervously tapping his pencil on the desk, the general lowered the tablet.

His eyes first rested on Julianna, who was quietly pacing back and forth. One might think after inhaling smoke and braving fire that she'd want to rest. That person would be wrong. Julianna Fregin wasn't the "resting" type. Maybe when she died, but Eddie was hopeful that wouldn't be for many centuries, if ever. Her current stunt proved that she had as many lives as a cat.

"Well?" asked Jack, his eyes expectant.

"Do you want the good news or the bad news first?" asked Lance. He had just returned from another of his classified missions.

"I always elect for the good news first," said Jack,

tapping the pencil as he pulled a yellow pad of paper to him.

Lance let out a long exhale. "ArchAngel only took minimal damage. The section that was hit can be repaired fairly quickly. The Intelligence Center will have to relocate to the bridge."

"That's mostly good news," said Eddie. "But Chester is going to be grumpy about it."

Lance consented with a nod. "Speaking of Chester, that whiz kid was able to get a whole *hell* of a lot of information when he hacked into Felix's accounts."

"That's good news, since we nearly got blown up doing it," said Eddie. He looked affectionately at Julianna. "Can you believe we snuck onto Felix's ship right under his nose? That guy has to be pissed."

"He's livid, based on what he tried to do to *ArchAngel*," said Jack.

"I fear that whatever Felix is planning, he's going to speed up the timeline now," said Lance.

"What *is* he planning?" asked Julianna, steering the conversation on course, as she was prone to doing.

"That," began Lance, "we don't know. However, Chester found information about a scientist by the name of Elemius Riley. He was contracted recently to create a drug for Felix."

"Elemius Riley," said Jack, combing his fingers over his chin. "The name rings a faint bell."

"It should," answered Lance. "He was a chief scientist involved in a few nanocyte projects."

"That's worrisome," said Julianna, alarm in her voice.

"Does Felix know that we have this information?" asked

Eddie. "Could he be going after Elemius to get to him before we do?"

Lance nodded, seeming to agree with this concern. "That was my question as well. Chester, that brilliant badass, apparently uploaded a nasty virus that covered his tracks when he was accessing *Unsurpassed's* database."

"Still, I don't think we should hesitate to track down this guy," urged Jack.

"Is that all the information that we have?" asked Julianna.

"Yes," answered Lance. "We know where Elemius can be found, but don't know what he created or how it could be used."

"So looks like we need to pay this guy a visit," said Eddie.

"That's exactly what I want you two to do," said Lance, leaning forward, placing both hands on the surface of the desk. "However, I want you to be careful. This individual has an impressive knowledge of nanocyte technology and he's been working for Felix. There's no telling what he's capable of or how well he's protected. I have to admit, I was more comfortable about the idea of you infiltrating *Unsurpassed* than going after an evil scientist who can do who-the-fuck-knows-what."

"Thanks for the concern, General," said Eddie. "We'll get what you need and then we can hopefully be one step ahead of Felix for once."

"Was that the bad news?" asked Jack. "About Elemius?"

"It's probably going to turn into a shit ton of bad news," said Lance and then motioned to Julianna and Eddie. "We'll find out more once they interrogate the scientist. However, no that's not actually the bad news."

Lance cleared his throat and looked at Julianna, a guilty expression on his face made the fine lines more pronounced. Then he swiveled his gaze to Eddie. "I handed this ship over to you both, but unfortunately, I'm going to need to take it back fairly soon."

"You're taking back *ArchAngel?*" asked Julianna. "What are *we* going to use?"

The look of guilt deepened. "*That,* I don't know yet. I'm on the hunt for something that will work. What Ghost Squadron does is important and I want you all to have the right ship, that's why I gave you *ArchAngel* in the first place. But I didn't foresee needing it back this soon."

"Whatever ship we get, can it have a bowling alley in it?" asked Eddie.

"I'll see what I can do," said Lance, rising to a standing position. "For now, your concern is going after Elemius. He's the next puzzle piece in this fucked up Felix mess."

"We won't let you down," said Julianna, straightening as she looked at the general.

19

Alpha-line Q-Ship, Planet Ronin, Behemoth System

"Do you really think this is all necessary?" asked Eddie, pulling at the helmet fastened under his chin.

"You heard the general," said Julianna, smoothing down her armor. She had to admit that the helmet wasn't exactly comfortable and made neck movement a bit cumbersome. However, she'd learned long ago not to question Lance's instincts. If he was worried about this Elemius character then it was for good reason.

"Okay, Pip is going to keep an eye on the ship, right?" asked Eddie.

"Eye on the ship," laughed Pip. "Yeah, you two toddle off and I'll house sit."

Julianna made to roll her eyes but smiled still. "It's cloaked anyway, and on the outskirts like this it should be fine." Doctor Elemius Riley lived in an old mansion on the fringe of a sprawling metropolis. Julianna was half grateful that they didn't have to venture into the city, but didn't like the idea of tiptoeing onto this guy's property. Something reeked of a trap, but she wasn't sure why.

"Knock-knock," said Eddie, readying himself in front of the hatch door.

Pip laughed again. "Who's there?"

"Ready," answered Eddie.

"Ready who?" asked Pip.

"Ready Eddie. Open up ole buddy, ole pal. We're ready to kick ass," said Eddie.

"Uhhhh…" said Julianna.

"I mean, question a civilian," corrected Eddie. "No ass kicking unless necessary."

"According to his file he sounds unassuming and scrawny," stated Pip.

"*You're* scrawny," retorted Julianna.

"I like to think that I've got wide shoulders, a barrel chest, muscular legs and a dimple on my left cheek," said Pip.

"Oh, you do, do you?" asked Julianna, amused.

"And I've got a larger than life personality," said Pip.

"And a giant head," added Julianna.

"And I'm modest too," said Pip as he opened the hatch. Beyond the ship were broken streets littered with trash and other debris. Most of the houses that lined the road were dilapidated, but at one time they had been large estates in pristine condition. Elemius's house was at the end of the road and the largest on the block.

Eddie and Julianna climbed from the Q-Ship, trying to be as inconspicuous as one could disembarking from a cloaked vehicle. Ronin was a strange planet, full of all sorts, about like their favorite Londil, Hatch. For that reason, they didn't look too out of place with their armor. Still the least amount of suspicion they stirred, the better.

Julianna was on high alert as they strode down the road. The yards were empty, and by the looks of it, so were most of the houses. The nearby metropolis was crammed with people and aliens of all sorts. That's where most had moved since Federation law had created jobs in the city.

They paced down the road, Eddie focused on one side of the street and Julianna on the other. It was strange to her to picture living in a house like this, one with windows and a roof and an outside yard. She'd adjusted to ship life so long ago that it was the norm. For most, not seeing sunlight or having open spaces with dirt was strange. For Julianna the opposite was true.

She stopped when they were outside of Elemius's wrought iron gate. It was unlocked, but that felt like a trap. Eddie reached out to unlatch it and Julianna found herself pushing him to the side.

"Hey," he complained, being bumped out of the way.

Julianna dismissed him with a wave and paused, her hand hovering over the handle for the gate. Finally she clamped down on the gate. Nothing happened. She was so sure that it was a trap.

I'm being paranoid, she thought as she pushed down, opening the gate lined with iron vines and leaves.

You're being protective, said Pip in her head.

Shush it. No one asked for your input.

Were you afraid the gate was going to electrocute the captain?

Why would I care if Teach got a little jolt of electricity? It wouldn't kill him.

True, but when we don't want someone to experience pain, however small, that's when we know we care about them and their general wellbeing.

Then what does it mean if I want to make you hurt?

I think it means we have an opportunity for self-love.

We? What, do you have a mouse in your pocket?

Pocket. Good one. I like the ideas of pockets. Maybe a fanny pack.

We're not having this conversation.

Indeed we are. Self-love is something that affects all relationships. You see, we can't love another until we love ourselves. When we have a good relationship with ourselves then we are ideally in a position to—

Shut. The. Fuck. Up.

Oh, said Pip, his voice tensing. **Such hostility.**

Julianna shook her head, crossing the long path between the gate and the house.

A tiny bell clinked overhead. Julianna knew better than to look up. Instead she shot off the path, scanning her surroundings. The yard was mostly brown, but still overgrown. Smoke sprang up from the ground, quickly cloaking their feet and legs.

"Hold your breath," said Julianna, covering her mouth.

It appears to just be steam, said Pip

Julianna relaxed, but didn't lower her hand.

Eddie's expression was almost unreadable since he was nearly covered in the steam. He waved his hand in front of his face, trying to wave away the mist.

"What the fuck?" he asked.

"I'm not sure," said Julianna, scanning the yard and

house and daring to look up. That's when she saw it. Directed at Eddie from nearby trees and light poles were six laser beams. He still stood on the path, although she couldn't really see where his feet were.

"Don't move, Teach," said Julianna, turning around, trying to figure out what weapon could be behind the lasers.

"What do you mean?" asked Eddie, looking down at his body. "The lasers are moving."

Julianna stole a glance at Eddie. He was right. The beams strobed over his legs, arms and torso, rotating like they were trying to find the right place on him to fire.

His head and heart were covered with the helmet and armor. He was probably fine, but still something about this made her nervous.

"Just don't move," said Julianna.

"Actually, you should back up and leave," said an unknown voice. Julianna tore her gaze in the direction of the porch, where the voice had come from. The porch and front section of the yard were covered in steam but she could make out a slender figure by the step. He wore a cold stare and held a gun of sorts. Something was off about the weapon, making it appear more like a tranquilizer gun.

"Are you Dr. Elemius Riley?" asked Eddie, holding his hands up in the air in surrender.

"I think you know I am, which is why you're about to die a slow death," said the man. He wore a crocheted sweater that made him appear older than he was with his brown hair and small eyes.

The lasers had stopped moving and were centered on

different parts of Eddie. Three were on his arms and the rest on his legs. "Uhhh…why the shots to the extremities?"

"Well, before you're shot in the arms and legs, I'm going to give you a shot of this," said Elemius, indicating the weapon in his hand. "That is, if you don't back up and leave. You *do* have a choice."

"We came for information," said Julianna, looking around.

The residence is empty aside from Elemius, said Pip.

That's a relief.

Not really. He has enough ammunition on the property to fight a small war.

Why, I wonder?

If you can get a bit closer to the house then I may be able to access his computer network.

I'm kind of hanging out here trying to keep Teach from getting shot.

Why do you care if he gets shot? He'll recover, right?

Shut it, Pip.

Elemius didn't at all look steady as he held the weapon, his eyes bouncing between Julianna and Eddie. "I'm not at liberty to give information."

Eddie shook his head. "Look, you can shoot me in the arm if you have to, but we're not really here for trouble."

"You're saying that because you're enhanced and don't worry about recovering from a bullet wound," said Elemius.

"Right," chuckled Eddie. "And our armor will lessen the blow."

Elemius waved the weapon up and down. "And what I

have here will make the blow exponentially worse. It will make it so that you don't recover quickly."

Oh fuck!

Get in there now, Julianna. I don't have a good feeling about this.

Julianna reached for her gun. She had it up and cocked before Elemius even registered the movement. She fired her pistol, her aim perfect. The bullet struck right above the weapon in Elemius's hand, making him drop it. Julianna sprinted over, kicking the weapon away as she simultaneously grabbed both of his lanky arms and tied them behind his back.

He bucked backwards, trying to knock his head into her face. However, he was fairly easy to control due to his lack of muscles.

"Let me...let me...let me go," yelled Elemius.

Julianna clamped his arms tightly together, nearly laughing at the miniscule effort the skinny scientist was exerting. Eddie joined her a moment later, zip tying his wrists together. When she was sure that Eddie had him, she stepped back, inspecting the weapon she'd kicked and landed at the bottom of the stair.

"What are you playing at, fool?" asked Eddie, pushing Elemius up against the side of the house so that his face was smashed against the brown siding.

"I'm not allowed to talk to you," he tried to say, his speech obscured by the wall.

"You worked on the nanocyte program for the Federation, is that right?" asked Julianna, eying the weapon. Up close, it really resembled a tranquilizer gun.

Elemius fought his restraints to no effect. "Check my files if you want."

"Who said we have access to that?" teased Eddie, barely using any effort to push Elemius into the wall.

"I know you're working for General Reynolds," said Elemius.

This got Julianna's attention. Her head popped up and she scowled at the weasel of a scientist. "How do you know that?"

"B-Because…" said Elemius, still squirming.

"Because isn't an answer. You should know that, doctor," said Eddie.

"Because Felix mentioned it, okay?" yelled Elemius.

Eddie shook his head, clicking his tongue. "Such a temper on this one. Why don't you tell us what you created for Felix, then I won't have to make you squirm anymore."

"I don't have to tell you anything," said Elemius, his legs shuffling around under him but his body staying firmly planted against the wall.

Eddie held up one finger and smiled. "This really pains me more than you." He then thrust the single finger into the scientist's ribs, goosing him in the side.

Elemius let out a loud sound of overwhelming pain. *Man, this guy is a real pushover,* thought Julianna.

Yes, but if my suspicions are correct, if he'd shot you with that weapon on the ground then you'd be a goner, said Pip.

Suspicions? What have you learned?

Not much. I got access to a journal of sorts. It references an anti-nanocyte technology he was working on called degen.

"Okay, fine," screamed Elemius. "I'll tell you this much. Felix is planning on attacking the general."

"Duh," said Eddie, shaking his head. "We already knew that." He pulled back his arm, almost in comedic style and then shot it into Elemius's ribs.

"Ouch!" yelled the scientist. "Fine, fine, fine! Stop it!" He wheezed for several seconds before snorting. Snot was dripping down from both of his nostrils.

"He's going to attack him in forty-eight hours on Onyx station. I'm not aware of the details, but I know how he plans on doing it," said Elemius.

"Attack him? On Onyx? That's impossible," said Eddie.

Elemius tried to shake his head. "No, not if he has the right weapon."

"The general is heavily guarded. There's no way he's getting close to him," argued Eddie.

"That's why he's going to cause a diversion. An attack on one of the housing units on the upper decks," said Elemius, still wheezing.

"I don't get how he thinks that will work. The general will still have security personnel," said Eddie.

"Right, and they'll take all the hits, which is what Felix planned for," said Elemius. "However, all he has to do is get one hit on him for his attack to work."

"Like a headshot?" asked Eddie.

Elemius tried to shake his head but still wasn't granted much room. "No, Felix wants him to suffer. He's taking him out the old-fashioned way."

"Old-fashioned way?" Eddie looked at Julianna, confused. "I don't get it."

Julianna bent over and picked up the weapon. There

was a single dart loaded into it. She pulled it loose and eyed it. "Old fashion as in...?"

"Yes," said Elemius, his words slurred. "A human death. And Felix can easily get off a shot of that from a dart gun, striking the general anywhere on his skin."

"What is that stuff?" asked Eddie, looking at Julianna curiously.

"Degen, apparently," she said. "Continue or my friend is going to make you soil yourself."

"B-b-but I'm cooperating," squired Elemius.

"Keep going," urged Julianna.

Elemius gulped. "Once the general is struck then he can die easily. A single shot. A blow to a major artery. Anything that would kill a non-enhanced human."

"So degen undoes the nanocyte technology," said Julianna, mostly to herself.

"Yes, and it can't be redone. Once General Lance is struck then he's human, the one thing that will make him normal. He'll die, unable to heal," explained Elemius.

"You have to tell us exactly how this degen works," ordered Eddie, pushing the scientist firmer into the wall, picking him off his feet.

"I can't!" said Elemius. "I've already told you enough. Felix is going to kill me."

"*We're* going to kill you," Eddie threatened.

"But I—"

"Don't bother with him," said Julianna, cutting him off. "We have a sample of the drug. We'll have our own guy study it."

Eddie nodded, pulled Elemius off the wall, making him teeter like a puppet, toes merely brushing the ground.

"Good plan. And in the meantime, this traitor can occupy our brig."

"What? No! I told you what you wanted," argued Elemius.

"Which is why we know you belong in the brig. Thanks, pal," joked Eddie as he tugged Elemius toward the ship.

20

Bridge, QBS *ArchAngel*, Behemoth System

Chester eyed the man who was plopped at the workstation next to his. *He chewed too loudly,* his jaw clicking every time he put a Cheeto in his mouth. Orange dust sprinkled from his lips and off his fingernails. The disgusting human being wiped his hands on his jeans, leaving behind an orange streak, before typing on his keyboard again.

Chester looked down at his own workstation, a temporary sorry-excuse-for-a-computer. He'd sanitized the keyboard the best he could but realized that it just needed to be torched. People were disgusting.

"Those things are going to kill you," said Chester to Jimmy or Bob or whatever the guy had said his name was.

"Huh?" the man said, looking at Chester.

"Those things," said Chester, pointing at the Cheeto about to enter the dumbass' mouth. "They are going to kill you."

The moron laughed before popping the Cheeto into his pie-hole. "They're chips, not crack. I think I'll be fine."

Chester's eyes dropped to the guy's gut that spilled over his skinny jeans, which were a horrible name given the person who was wearing them. His hairy stomach stretched the shirt he wore to a dangerous capacity and peeked out at the bottom. "It's more of a cumulative thing. That's what I'd worry about if I were you."

"I'm not certain that I asked your advice," said Sponge-Bob, who also had bucked teeth that matched his crooked nose.

"Not certain, huh? Like there's a probability that you might have asked and can't recollect?" asked Chester, his tone patronizing. It was a style he'd perfected as a self-proclaimed loather of most of the universe's population.

SpongeBob didn't seem to know the answer to this, having been stumped by a series of new words. Slowly he lifted a Cheeto and deposited it into his mouth. "Chris, we have to sit together for a while. We should try and get along."

"Name is Chester Wilkerson, Cheetos. Would you mind not spraying orange dust all over me? Unlike you, I have a certain level of cleanliness I prefer."

"Hey dude, why don't you—"

"Oh, Chester, you're so funny," said Marilla, sliding in between the workstations, partially blocking SpongeBob from view. She turned to the guy, looking at him over her shoulder. "Don't be offended, Jimmy, his sense of humor is an acquired taste."

"Yeah, alright, Marilla," said Jimmy. He fastened his headphones over his ears, securing them on his giant head.

Marilla turned back to Chester, venom in her eyes like he had never seen before. "Is there a reason you're trying to make everyone on the bridge hate you?"

"Am I? Oh good," said Chester. "It's working. And quite simply, I'm doing it because I don't play well with others."

Marilla placed her hand on Chester's desk and leaned down, her voice a hush. The bridge was mostly full, the captain and the commander having filled many positions. "You don't have to work with these people. Just do your job at this workstation."

"But they are all lurking around me with their bad smells and loud chewing," said Chester, fashioning a pouting look on his face.

Marilla glanced around at the various workstations. "Yeah, I totally get it. That girl over there chews her gum like a jackhammer."

Chester beamed. "See, you and I are two of the same."

"Still you could try a little diplomacy," suggested Marilla. "It wouldn't kill you to ignore the bad behavior instead of pointing it out and insulting the crew."

"Wouldn't it though?" asked Chester. "Have you *seen* that guy eat Cheetos? It's disgusting."

Marilla turned to watch as SpongeBob crammed a handful of Cheetos into his mouth, like they were stranded passengers fighting for space on a life boat. Again, he wiped his hand covered in orange dust on his jeans and resumed typing.

Marilla turned back and shivered with disgust. "Just try and stay busy and not give him notice."

"If you so desire it, dear Mar," said Chester.

"Hey there," a girl said. She was about their age, early

twenties. She wore skinny jeans, but was actually thin, unlike Cheetos Breath. Her long blonde hair hung over one shoulder and she had that bubbly look about her.

Marilla's face contorted with a grimace, probably without her consent. "Uhhh…hey, Amanda. What do you need?"

"Nothing from you," the girl said. She turned and batted her eyelashes at Chester. "I was wondering if you'd look at my computer. It appears to be malfunctioning."

"Chester is an Intelligence Officer, not tech support," stated Marilla, her tone annoyed.

"I know that," said Amanda. "I just thought since he's right here and my station is over there that it made sense."

"It's fine," said Chester, stretching to a standing position. He'd been sitting for too long. "I'll take a look."

"But you have all the data from *Unsurpassed* to sort through," argued Marilla.

"He said he'd do it, alright?" Amanda said, cutting in.

Marilla was giving Chester a look that meant so much to him. She cared. More importantly, she was jealous. "It's fine, Mar. Remember…diplomacy."

She seethed deeper as he followed Amanda to her crumb-filled workstation. People really were disgusting pigs.

Eddie watched the interaction between Chester and Marilla and the other team members with mild interest. He might have appeared like a brute with little emotional intelligence, but that was more of a façade he'd perfected over the years.

"You're staring," said Julianna, sidling up next to him.

He offered her a sideways smile. "They wouldn't know I was watching them if I held up a giant sign."

"Well, update me on what's going on, since I've been busy working," said Julianna, appearing amused as she watched the young adults. Youngsters must appear like aliens to her since it had been so long since she'd been new to this world. Was it impossible for Julianna to relate to anyone? Eddie didn't think so.

"How did the interrogation go?" asked Eddie.

"Elemius is a sniveling little jerk," said Julianna.

"So he wouldn't give you a breakdown of his formula," guessed Eddie.

"Oh, he probably would, but I decided he wasn't worth my time," said Julianna. "I think Hatch can give us something more reliable. I interrogated the scientist enough to find out that he's offered us most of the useful information he has."

"So then we have a date on Onyx station in a couple of days," said Eddie and then gauging the look of mortification on Julianna's face he added, "The team, I mean. Fletcher's team and us."

"Yes," said Julianna, clearing her throat uncomfortably. "The general has been informed. He laughed when I told him what Felix had planned."

"What did he say?" asked Eddie. Of course, the general laughed when informed about an assassination attempt on his life.

"He said it was a genius effort that Felix had put into

the plan and he wished the fucking twit would have put the same energy into something that contributed to the universe at large," said Julianna.

"Well put," said Eddie, his focus returning to Chester, who was bent over the young Communication Officer's desk.

"And he also said that he couldn't wait to see the fuck-tard's face when his plan failed," said Julianna.

"Yes, and then we'll have secured another threat and maybe we can take a day off," said Eddie, still watching the pair on the other side of the bridge.

"We both know that when you cut a head off of the beast, that nine more just grow," stated Julianna.

"Oh, a little hydra reference," said Eddie, rocking forward and back on his toes. "I like it."

Julianna eyed him, a bit of surprise on her face. "How did you get a hydra reference?"

"Honestly, Jules, I'm not just a pretty face," said Eddie, teasingly. "I know things."

"You hide it well," said Julianna.

"Like for instance," said Eddie, indicating Chester helping Amanda with her computer. "Amanda doesn't want to ask Gary, our computer tech, for help because the last time she did he hit on her. Amanda doesn't fancy Gary because she doesn't fancy guys."

"Did you just say the word 'fancy?'" asked Julianna, cutting in.

"I did," said Eddie, laughing inside. He nodded his head at Marilla. "And then we have Marilla and Chester, who are about as perfectly matched as two people can be."

"But...?" asked Julianna.

Eddie smiled at her intuition. "But Marilla is a no nonsense type and doesn't want to risk her career over what could be a passing flame."

"And Chester?" asked Julianna.

"Well, Chester would delete the entire Dark Web for Marilla, but he's still playing his cards close to his chest. He understands he's got time on his side."

"How do you know all this?" asked Julianna.

Eddie shrugged. "I'm observant. Most people wear their emotions on the outside if you know where to look."

"Eddie…" said Julianna, her voice careful.

"Yes?" he asked, turning to face her directly, taking his focus off of the crew members for the first time in a while.

"Pip is afraid you've got a fever," said Julianna, a grin spreading on her face. "However, I told him I'm more concerned that you've been taken over by a strange alien who is using your body as a host."

"Ha-ha, you two," said Eddie. "I'll just keep my observations to myself. Now you can see why I have in the past."

"Because of the incessant teasing?" guessed Julianna.

"Well, and it makes others nervous if they realize you can read them so well," stated Eddie.

Julianna dropped her gaze in the way she did when she was having an argument with Pip. It's like she went away during those conversations.

"What is Pip saying?" asked Eddie.

Julianna looked up, startled for a moment, but then covered the expression. "He, uhhh… He said he would like to see what goes on in your head."

"Oh, well, *there's* an idea I hadn't considered," said

Eddie. Having an AI in his head would be the ultimate upgrade.

"It's *an* idea. A horrible one that we're not considering," said Julianna, dismissively. She twisted around and looked out at the bridge. "What makes Marilla and Chester the perfect couple, I'm just wondering?" She added the last part with a bit of hesitation.

"That's easy," said Eddie, finding Marilla with his gaze, who was working a bit distractedly at her station. Her eyes kept drifting to Chester as he helped Amanda. "Opposites don't attract. It's quite the *opposite*. Get it?" He gave her a wink and she rolled her eyes. "However," he continued, "I think the other person needs to have a bit of something to balance out their partner. So Chester and Marilla have a similar work ethic, they're both incredibly intelligent and masters in their fields. But they have different areas of expertise. And whereas Chester is outgoing, Marilla is introverted. She's level-headed and he's flippant. It's a delicate balance, but those two seem to fit the bill, about like my parents. We'll just see if they figure it out."

"Your face just changed," said Julianna.

"I did just give a speech," admitted Eddie trying to act dismissive, although he knew what Julianna meant. He felt the lines press into his forehead at the mention of his parents.

"You miss them, don't you?" she asked, referring to Eddie's folks.

"Every damn day," he said before he could stop himself.

"And the regret? What about that? It's always in your eyes when you speak about them. You realize I can read it on you, the same way you read other people, right?" asked Julianna.

Eddie looked directly at her. What was the point in entirely trying to hide it if she could plainly see the scars written in his expression? "I think someone as seasoned as you knows it takes a lifetime to understand our past."

21

QBS *ArchAngel*, Cargo Bay, Behemoth System

I bet you were glad that ArchAngel interrupted when she did, said Pip in Julianna's head.

You shouldn't gamble. You'll lose, answered Julianna.

I wager that the captain was glad for the timing of this meeting, too.

Julianna strode beside Eddie toward Hatch's lab. ArchAngel had in fact interrupted the conversation on the bridge to tell them that the doctor had information for them. It was a good thing Pip couldn't read her emotions, because then he'd know she was intrigued by the conversation with Eddie and not at all happy about the timing of the interruption. Julianna was practiced at blocking when necessary, which she'd found she had to do more and more with Pip since he became sentient.

Maybe it was the near death experience or the upgrade, but Eddie was changing. Or maybe he was just showing more of himself to her. That happens after fighting in battle alongside others. The memories of the bonds she'd formed through deathly missions flashed across her mind, making her remember. Remember many of the things she worked to forget…

Pip, why don't you busy yourself with some online poker, since you like to gamble so much lately. Only play with fake money though.

I play slots when you're sleeping. There's a site that I found that doubles your chips if you send them referrals.

How are you sending them referrals?

I'm a man who owns many hats.

You're not a man at all.

Of sorts, then.

And that's what you do when I sleep? Can't you find something more productive?

There was a moment of silence. **I've considered all options and no, that's the best use of my time on most nights. It helps me to hone my understanding of random number generators, which you should know, pretty much keeps this universe going round and round.**

Random number generators? That's what you suppose runs this giant ship we call life?

Good analogy and yes, in a way. They explain so much. There's no randomness in life. It's about energy and the generators even prove it. Slots prove it. Hell, shuffling your playlist proves it.

I don't have a playlist.

You do now. I've created different ones for battles, workouts, sleeping. Whatever you want, just name it. That's another way I spend my nights.

You're very strange.

I've also been studying knitting and crocheting techniques but I haven't gotten very far with the hobby.

Because you don't have hands?

Bingo.

"Why don't you want to share Pip?" asked Eddie, cutting into their conversation.

"Believe me when I tell you that I'm saving your sanity, which I'm losing increasingly," said Julianna, waving to Hatch as they crossed the floor of the cargo area.

You know I keep you entertained.

I don't know what you're talking about, actually.

You love me, sang Pip. **You don't wanna share me.**

I'm a soldier charged with protecting humanity. You're a virus I'm trying not to allow to spread.

"But I have spread," said Pip overhead in the cargo area. *That's right.* Julianna had forgotten that Hatch had made it so that Pip could interface with the Q-Ships, comms, and his main work areas.

Hatch's eyes darted up to the ceiling. "Spread what?"

Julianna waved him off. "Pip is trying to be cute but doesn't realize he's a runt troll who needs to cuddle up and shush it."

"I think trolls are cute," said Pip.

Knox laughed as he worked on one of the new Q-Ships. He'd put on weight, filling out his cheeks and making him look healthy. Before he'd been underfed and pasty, but a few hours in the Kezza sun looked to have been good for him.

"I had a chance to review the sample of degen that you

brought back and have a report," said Hatch, waddling over.

"In record time," said Eddie. "You said it would take you at least a day."

"Under promise and over deliver," muttered Hatch, stretching his tentacle over to a far workstation and picking up a vial of purple gel liquid.

"Does it do what Elemius said it does?" asked Julianna.

Hatch's expression dropped into one of dead seriousness. "Let me put it this way: you should have never chanced touching the degen."

"Really?" asked Julianna.

"My calculations state that the substance is incredibly concentrated and only a small amount would undo your nanocytes' programming," said Hatch.

"And it's not reversible?" asked Eddie.

"If you mean can you go back into a Pod-doc to fix the virus, then no. I only know of one such cure for the virus and I'm holding it right now," said Hatch, waving the vial in the air.

"You had time to create an antidote," said Eddie with a whistle. "When does this guy sleep?"

"I'm still trying to figure that out," said Knox, wiping sweat from his brow with the back of his arm.

"Never mind, you two," said Hatch, stretching his tentacle and wagging the anti-serum in front of Julianna's face. "This is your only chance to undo the degen virus if Felix strikes the general with it."

She grabbed the vial, clutching it tightly in her fingers. "Only chance? This was the only one you created? Can't we get more?"

"I'd love to make you more. I really would," said Hatch, shaking his head at Knox who looked to be covering a nervous smile.

"Is it because we only got one sample of the degen?" asked Eddie. "Maybe we can go back and get more from Elemius or get him to talk about the composition."

Hatched waved him off with his tentacle. "I'm fairly certain I have the composition documented correctly."

"What do you need from us in order to make more of the anti-serum?" asked Julianna. "I don't feel comfortable with only one. What if the general is struck more than once? We need to be prepared."

"I agree, but that's all you have and all you're getting," said Hatch. "Note that if the general is struck with degen that he has minutes to take this antidote. If he doesn't then it won't reverse the effects. Also, one of you need to be prepared to catch him after he takes it because it will knock him out. It's a cure all, but kind of like the Pod-doc, it's going to put him in a comatose state for a while."

Julianna nodded to this but not all of this computed.

"But if you created one dose, can't you create another?" asked Eddie, looking as perplexed as Julianna felt.

"Hatch, is it a time conflict? Maybe if we delay the general's schedule then we can stall the attack," said Julianna.

Hatch looked at Knox who was hard at work on the Q-Ship, or at least making a good show of it. "Gunner, why don't you inform these two what they'd need to supply me with if they wanted more antiserum?"

The young mechanic slid out from under the ship all the way and looked up at the three from the ground.

"Remember the vermis rex? That's what the doctor would need to make more of the formula." Knox covered his laughter by pushing himself back under the Q-Ship.

"Oh," chirped Eddie, looking guilty. "So that's how you made this?" He pointed to the vial clutched in Julianna's hand.

"Exactly," said Hatch. "And we're lucky we had enough for this. That's exactly one dose of the cure. Take any less and it's not going to work. The degen will forever plague your internal system."

"Okay, well we're going to have to make this work, then," said Julianna, trying to project hope in her voice. They hadn't bet on having a cure, so this was actually better than they expected. However, there were so many unknown variables in this mission and Felix's weapons made her and Eddie incredibly vulnerable.

One shot. That's all it would take to turn everything around, making them forever, purely human.

22

Alpha-line Q-Ship, Docking Station, Onyx Station, Paladin System

Julianna secured the vial of antiserum in her armored vest. She'd be the closest to General Lance Reynolds and therefore in the best position to deliver him the cure for degen. But that was a worst case scenario. They had a strong plan. *Diversion.* That was key. Felix didn't know that they had wind of his plan and would be retaliating with force and strategy. Hopefully he was knocked on his ass and sent running with his tail pinched tightly between his boney legs. Or he'd blow up Onyx Station, not even caring for his own life if he could take down the general.

"Carnivore, this is Strong Arm. Do you copy?" Julianna said over the comms.

"Copy, Strong Arm," said Lars at once over the comms.

"What's your status?" she asked.

"We're almost in position," said Lars.

It was chancy, but a risk the general wanted to take.

Chester had used the same navigation tracker to find *Unsurpassed*, but only using it briefly, hoping that its position didn't shift too much. He unsurprisingly found that it was parked close to Onyx station, hiding behind a tiny moon.

Lars and the rest of the flight crew were now en route to surround the ship, at a safe distance. The last thing the Federation needed was for *Unsurpassed* to join the fight if things got ugly. According to Hatch, the ship had enough fire power to do major damage to the station. Felix might resort to drastic actions when he learned his plans had been compromised.

"Remember to keep attacks to a minimum," said Julianna over the comm. "Distract *Unsurpassed*. Draw the ship away, but try not to inflict too much damage. We want that ship intact."

"Copy that, Strong Arm," said Lars. "We're officially in position with the target in our sights."

"Good work, Carnivore," said Eddie, strapping his side arm into his holster. "We'll get you a steak when this is all over."

"The bloodier, the better," said Lars, his voice light.

"Gross," said Eddie, grimacing with disgust at Julianna. "He's like a vampire."

"Lizard vamp," said Julianna, agreeing.

"What a bizarre combination," said Eddie.

The pair watched as Fletcher's team filed out of the Q-Ship. The lieutenant strode over, saluting to Eddie and Julianna. "My team will divide into three groups, protecting the areas we discussed. Any last minute orders?"

"Protect the people," stated Julianna. "That's key. We can't let Felix escape unless it means saving lives."

"The blue team has already been dispersed to evacuate the areas marked for attack," said Fletcher.

"Good work," said Eddie. "We're on the main channel. Communicate with us about your progress."

"Yes, sir," said Fletcher.

Julianna turned to face Eddie who had an extra pack strapped to his back. "Are you ready to get dressed?"

"Yes, I'm ready," said Eddie and then paused, his eyes carrying a great seriousness in them. "Commander, I know you think I have the dangerous job, but we're both in compromised positions because of that degen weapon."

"So be careful, right? That's what you're going to say next, isn't it?" asked Julianna.

"Well, yeah, but there's something else," said Eddie and then he fell silent, hesitation heavy in his expression.

"What is it?" asked Julianna, her pulse pounding with adrenaline.

Eddie shook his head. "It doesn't matter. Never mind. Just be careful. You're a badass, but there's a mad man out there who can undo all that."

Julianna laughed. "You think I'm only badass because of the Pod-doc? You should have met me before I was enhanced."

Eddie chuckled. "Man, I'm such an asshole. Of course, you were strong before. Now you're just more so."

"Yeah, whatever," said Julianna, disembarking from the Q-Ship.

Upper Decks, Onyx Station, Paladin System

When they'd discussed strategy, Julianna had been the practical one, urging the general to cut Felix off before the attack. That was the right approach. Why let a tyrant kick off his evil plans when he could be preemptively shut down?

Jack knew better, though. Felix had been planning this for too long. Over the last two days no suspicious ships had docked at Onyx station, meaning that Felix had put everything into place before they brought Elemius into custody.

Eddie shut himself into a side room on the far side of the office that General Reynolds held. He was surrounded by Federation security. That was supposed to make him feel better. They were the best, after all, so why was he worried? Felix hadn't dared an assassination on the general until he'd created a virus that ensured his attacks were fatal. That's because it was unlikely that the security would ever fail at protecting the general. But Felix had thought of almost everything, with his attack on the upper decks. In a normal scenario, security would be thinned in order to fight back. But Felix wasn't counting on Fletcher's team being in place.

Eddie opened his pack and stared down. He gulped. This had never been a strategy that he considered, but it did make sense. Somewhere, two other members of General Reynold's security team were opening similar packs.

"I'm in position, Blackbeard," chimed Julianna's voice over the comm.

"Okay," said Eddie. He found himself momentarily frozen, staring at the contents of the pack.

"You there, Blackbeard?" asked Julianna.

"Yeah," said Eddie. "Inform the general that we are on schedule and all four should rendezvous at the established time."

"Copy that," said Julianna.

Upper Decks, Onyx Station, Paladin System

Clearing out the floors hadn't been the concern for Fletcher. The bulk of his forces had been doing it without causing any red flags. If Felix's team had seen shop owners and residents moved out, then they'd know that their plan had been leaked. The team had managed to do it quietly, sneaking out the civilians without causing any disturbances. Now the decoys were in place, but not knowing when the strike would happen was a mounting stress that worsened with each long, passing minute.

"Stay in position," said Fletcher over the comm to his team.

These were men and women that he'd served with in the heat of battle. Some of them he'd known for over a decade. And all of them he'd die to protect if it came to that. He always prayed that it didn't, but nothing was ever guaranteed.

Instead, Chad Fletcher relied on the same mentality his father whispered to him before he left on missions for the Federation. "While I'm gone, son, keep your chin up, eyes open, and mouth shut."

The first time his father told him that, Fletcher looked at him with confusion. The old man knelt next to his small cot and smiled, seeming to understand his son's confusion. "I mean: confidence, observation and deliberation, son. The man who is sure of himself can lead others. The man who is keen will always find the solution. And when we're quiet, that's when we hear what most choose to speak over."

Fletcher's father had said that to him a total of thirty-two times before he failed to return from a mission. His dad had come back from more assignments than most in his squadron. He was a small legend among the Special Operation teams. Fletcher hoped he would make him proud one day and live up to his name.

Chin up, eyes open, and mouth shut, he thought to himself.

Upper Deck, Onyx Station, Paladin System

Julianna watched as the general paced back and forth. She knew he was a bit less fidgety than before when he smoked cigars. It made sense to her that smoking a cigar would relieve some of the nervous tension. However, she respected the general for more than his decision to quit smoking. He'd signed off on this plan, although it involved his attendance.

When offered a different solution, he said, "Goddamn it! You think I'm going to allow a bunch of honorable men and women to risk their lives because a dick-ass wants me dead? If they're fighting, then I am, too. If Felix wants to kill me, then let him damn well try. I can't wait to see the fucktard's face when his plan fails."

"The captain says he's in position," said Julianna, relaying Eddie's confirmation over the comm.

"And the other security personnel?" asked Lance.

Julianna nodded. "Ready, sir."

"Now we just wait for the attack to start," said Lance.

"Yes, per protocol, we will move you to a safe room as soon as the message is relayed. Until then, we'll stick to the schedule we'd normally follow," said Julianna.

"I'm not happy that we have to allow an attack to happen on the upper decks for this all to go to plan," said Lance, still pacing.

"Yes, me either. But Jack assured me this was the best way to pull Felix out of hiding. Otherwise, he's going to split and he has too many things in place that he could possibility get away," said Julianna.

Lance nodded. "I trust Jack." A moment later the general added. "More importantly, I trust you, Commander Fregin."

She smiled, unable to hide the pride she felt from hearing the words. "Thank you, sir. I'm honored."

Upper Deck, Onyx Station, Paladin System

Fletcher stared out at the long corridor that was flanked by different doors and pipes that ran to various residences. In the distance, he made out the shape of two figures, both dressed in long coats, their heads obstructed by frilly hats. Many of the upper class women on Onyx wore dresses similar to this. No one would suspect under those hats were incredibly skilled Special Ops soldiers.

"An explosive has been detected," said a voice over the comm.

"Location?" asked Fletcher, pressing back into the shadows.

"Second section, door eight," answered the scout soldier. "Perimeter is clear."

"Good work," said Fletcher. "Time of detonation?"

Before an answer came a loud explosion rocked the floor, sending Fletcher backward. He paused, flexing every one of his muscles. The team around him did the same, staying upright and on alert.

From the north end of the deck, running footsteps thundered, audible over the explosions. It had to be the pirates Felix had planted as a diversion. They probably thought they were going to stroll onto this deck, dripping with riches and finery, and loot and have fun. *Fuck these guys.*

"Hold your position," ordered Fletcher.

The women carrying designer handbags and shoes screamed, holding up their hands as if in surrender. *They are great actors*, thought Fletcher.

The first set of pirates, a pair of Kezzin bandits, were on the women, pushing them into the wall. One grabbed their purses. It was incredibly hard for Fletcher to watch this go down and not intervene. However, he knew timing was key. Felix had to think that his distraction had gone off without a hitch. In a typical scenario of terrorism, the Federation security would be deployed, pulling forces away from other areas. That was the point. However these assfaces weren't expecting Fletcher's team to intervene.

Another set of pirates--a couple of thuggish-looking

Trid--slammed into several doors in the long corridor, breaking into multiple residences.

Fletcher held up his hand, fist clenched. *Confidence, observation, and deliberation.* He took in a deep breath and counted to four. Everything in front of him slowed as he focused.

Through the chaos, he watched as Nona threw off her frilly hat and swung around, knocking the Kezzin across the face. Her partner followed suit, slamming her elbow into the torso of the pirate behind her.

The two Trid turned and took notice, pulling guns from their waist.

Fletcher threw his fist forward. *"Now,"* he commanded over the comms, sending the team behind him and the one stationed on the other side into the fight. He sprinted ahead, slamming into the nearest Trid who was still facing the other direction.

A sea of bullets flew through the hall, each with its own target. In a single moment, multiple bodies fell against the corridor floor, collapsing like a field of wheat under the blade of a scythe.

One of the Trid rushed Fletcher, extending its rifle and attempting to fire. Fletcher bent to his side, avoiding the shot as he rolled. Before the Trid could try again, Fletcher sprung forward and slammed the butt of his rifle into the alien's breathing device, located on its hip.

The Trid wheezed, a sudden panic in its eyes. It fell to the floor, dropping the weapon right in front of Fletcher.

The first encounter was over in a matter of seconds. Fletcher only hoped the rest would be so easy.

Upper Deck, Onyx Station, Paladin System

"Detonation on Deck Twenty-five," said Julianna, picking up the transmission from Fletcher's team.

"Then it's time to move," said the general, lifting his chin and striding forward. Two guards took the position in front of him. Julianna pivoted and strode on one side of the general as two more guards marched at their back.

"Captain, we're moving into position," said Julianna over the comms.

"Copy that, Commander," said Eddie, his voice tight.

Julianna swallowed, feeling a constriction in her own throat. She paused when the general did, waiting for the guards to check the corridor outside of his office. More guards were stationed in the outer passageways.

The safe room, as Felix was probably well aware due to his extensive planning, was on the left. The intersection was cast in black, which would seem like a security concern if it wasn't for the fact that it was planned. Filtered light flickered overhead, as if the lights were malfunctioning. There was enough light to make out figures but no details.

Lance halted in the large intersection of corridors, making brief eye contact with a man who stood in the shadows. He nodded once and then turned sharply to the left, going in the opposite direction of the safe room.

***

The general's uniform fit perfectly, and gave Eddie a false sense of superiority. He was not General Lance Reynolds, even if he did wear his uniform. He was Edward Teach, a pilot…and sometimes a screwup. He preferred being the former. Maybe one day he wouldn't think of himself as a screwup. Maybe after today, should everything turn out okay.

Each mission carried with it the opportunity for redemption.

Eddie didn't really look like the general, even with the hair dye and uniform. But in the darkened intersection of corridors, he looked *close enough*, and that's what counted. The other two guards, dressed similarly, didn't look exactly like the general, either, but they were a damn close match. Hopefully they wouldn't see any action from all of this. They were mostly extra precautions in case Felix became suspicious.

The general paused in the intersection, the flickering light making shadows on his serious face. He nodded once at Eddie and then pivoted and marched toward the "actual" safe room.

There were still so many unknown factors, and yet everything was going to plan. One of those unknowns was how Felix would attack. There were a multitude of possibilities and therefore difficult to account for them all. But one thing was certain. He'd be damned surprised when he realized he had the wrong man.

As the guards dressed as the general crossed paths, Eddie turned, taking the corridor where the real Lance should be headed.

Julianna split from the general, following behind Eddie.

The corridor they entered was flickering with light as well, making it hard to see details. The supposed safe room was up ahead, which meant the attack had to come from one of the upcoming intersections. Although they were well guarded, there had to be something they were missing. An angle they hadn't considered.

Angle, thought Julianna.

Angle, what do you think it means? Asked Pip.

Julianna jerked her head up, squinting to see better. There were vents that ran continuously along the corners of the corridor.

Pip, the vent system above us! How large is it? Could it have been breached?

It's three by two feet and I'm scanning for intrusions now...

Hurry, Julianna urged, marching behind Eddie. At the next intersection, guards on either side saluted "the general."

On your right. There's an intruder in the ventilation system on the right.

"Be on guard!" yelled Julianna, alerting the soldiers. Shots behind them rang out, knocking the guards to the ground. An explosion in the neighboring corridor knocked out another of the guards. Julianna pushed Eddie forward as the darts kept raining down. Felix didn't want to just shoot the general. He wanted to change him and then kill him. He wasn't satisfied unless he made him suffer.

Darts hit the ground at Julianna's feet. She wheeled around, shooting at the vents where the darts were originating. One flew and nicked her in the shoulder. It didn't pierce the armor so she kicked backwards, urging Eddie down the corridor. The hatch door to the safe room was just ahead.

Another dart struck into the top of Julianna's boot. She rapidly fired, finally breaking through the grating. Just one more shot and she'd have this bastard.

The next dart passed by Julianna's arm that was holding her gun. She fired off another round and then there was a thud and creaking sound. Part of the ceiling collapsed and from the venting a body fell, hitting the ground in a crumpled mess. Julianna let out a sigh of relief, still on guard. *Something* had taken out the guards.

More gunfire rang out, exploding from either corridor. Julianna turned to Eddie just as Pip sounded in her head.

We have a problem!

What is it? The sniper with degen is dead.

It was too late. You were str—

Julianna frowned in confusion. The expression on Eddie's face made her even more befuddled. His mouth was gaping open and his eyes staring at her gun.

Everything slowed down. Sounds were drawn out like they were being played at a reduced speed. Her vision was forced into slow motion. It then blurred. Her hearing deadened then everything was too faint. The noises she'd heard before were indistinct to her. All at once her body felt heavier, less agile, like she'd just run a marathon and her muscles were fatigued. She hadn't known fatigue since…

Panic swept through her mind at once. She looked down at her gun, wondering what she'd see. Knowing it already.

Pip! Pip! Julianna screamed in her own head.

But he didn't answer.

Julianna's gun looked the same. She turned it over and then she saw it. *The dart.* It was stuck into the top of her hand at the bottom of her wrist. Without thinking she pulled the dart containing degen from her hand and let it fall, clattering to the floor.

Somewhere she was aware of a fight that was being fought.

Gun shots. Explosions. The general. It all flashed at the front of her mind and then quickly receded. After all these decades, Julianna…was normal. She was purely human. Completely vulnerable. She was going to die. A simple gunshot wound. A simple virus. A fall. Any of it could kill her. All at once she realized how much she'd taken for granted. She had been enhanced for so long that she had forgotten what it was like to be normal, to be average, to be a regular human.

Eyes wide, Julianna looked up at Eddie. His face communicated the same shock. They needed to get him to the safe room. They needed to lure Felix away from the general. They needed to—

Eddie darted forward and pulled at the side of Julianna's vest. She couldn't figure out what he was doing. Why was he yanking at her armor? Then he pulled the purple vial from her secure pocket, his hands steady but eyes buzzing.

"No!" Julianna said at once, realizing what he intended for her to do. "No, no, no," she repeated.

"Yes," Eddie insisted, thrusting the vial of liquid at her after removing the plug. "You have to. Otherwise—"

"That's for the general," argued Julianna.

Where was Pip? She felt so alone without him in her head. Of course with the degen virus she couldn't interface with Pip. That was only a functionality made possible due to the nanocytes.

"You've been hit," Eddie insisted. "You remember what Hatch said. The antidote has to be taken immediately."

"But the general… If I take that then Lance has no option," said Julianna.

Eddie looked up in the direction of the gun fire in the distance. It was a cacophony of indistinguishable noises to Julianna, without her enhanced hearing. "We're going to defend the general so he won't need it," argued Eddie. "Someone is coming. Take it now." Eddie pushed the vial into Julianna's hands.

Of course, she had a choice, but it also felt as though she didn't. If she took the antidote then she might be the reason General Reynolds didn't recover if he was struck. But if he wasn't struck and she didn't take it then it would all be for nothing. The thought of never talking to Pip in her head made the rest of her lifetime, however much longer she lived, seem lonely and cold. *How much she'd taken for granted.*

Julianna gripped the vial and tossed it back in one movement. The sludge-like liquid was cold, although it had been in her pocket. It tasted disgusting, and coated her mouth at once. Then she remembered that it was comprised of the gross slime the *vermis rex* had spit at her. She coughed and nearly gagged on the chunky liquid. With great effort she swallowed, working it down her throat.

"All of it," said Eddie.

Julianna tried to nod, but her legs gave out under her.

Just as Hatch had said, she was quickly losing consciousness. Was that a sign that the antidote had worked and that she'd awaken to find herself back to normal? She desperately hoped so. Julianna gulped down the rest of the liquid, only slightly conscious of Eddie's eyes, wide with alarm and nerves as he stared past her at the long corridor masked in smoke and filled with loud sounds.

She wanted to turn around and see what was approaching—or who—but her weight dragged her down as the antidote overtook her. She reached out to steady herself on Eddie's shoulder, but missed. Julianna fell, to the ground but before she landed arms caught her. They wrapped around her back, then lifted her legs.

Her head cradled against Eddie's chest. Her eyes fell shut, unable to stay open as he carried her away.

23

Upper Deck, Onyx Station, Paladin System

There were more pirates than Fletcher had expected. How had these guys snuck onto Onyx station? This must have been Felix's influence.

"We're surrounded," one of his soldiers called over the comm.

"Same here," another exclaimed.

Retreating was always an option. Or he could call for backup from Federation security. However, taking care of this without involving the Federation directly was best. They needed to focus on the general. Fletcher's team was supposed to handle the pirates.

Fletcher knew he needed to say something. It was his decision to make. But there was something he was missing. He blinked, looking out at the smoke-filled corridor streaked with gun fire and explosions.

Fletcher felt like he was fighting Mamaths again, who

were nearly impossible to defeat. As soon as one of them fell, three more thundered out of the frozen forest.

An idea hit him so hard that he wanted to double over in giddy laughter. *Of course! Why hadn't he thought of it before?*

"Pip, are you there?" Fletcher asked over the comm.

"Yes, Lieutenant," said Pip, a hint of sadness in his voice.

Fletcher dismissed it. "Can you hook into the thermostat for this deck?"

"I'm already connected," said Pip at once.

"Make it fucking *cold*," ordered Fletcher.

"Copy that, Lieutenant," said Pip.

Immediately a rush of frigid cold air flowed from the vents, spraying Fletcher in the face. "Bundle up, team. It's about to get frosty." Fletcher turned his attention to a group of Trids who had overpowered one of his team members. "I want you all to focus your efforts on the remaining Trids. The Kezzin aren't going to be a problem for us anymore. They'll be statues."

A collective "Yes, sir" came over the comm. Fletcher had remembered how hot the planet Kezza had been, and also how stiffly Lars had moved when on Klamath. After deliberating on it he decided that the Kezzin couldn't stand cold temperatures and that's exactly how they were going to secure their footing in this battle. Around them, the Kezzin started to freeze up, their reflexes now too slow to counter the attacks of his team.

The soldiers swept the room, making quick work of the frigid Kezzin.

Fletcher moved in, slamming a knee into the closest Kezzin guard and sending him into the wall. The Kezzin fell to the floor, doubled over, shaking from the cold and writhing in pain.

In a matter of seconds, the team had disabled them, ready to focus their energy on the remaining Trid.

Several of the shark-like aliens swarmed the team. Fletcher was ready, swinging his rifle around and unloading three quick shots at two of the soldiers. The first fell, wounded in the abdomen, while the second continued to charge, ready with its weapon aimed.

The enemy fired, shooting at Fletcher, hitting him directly in the shoulder. The body armor absorbed the bulk of the blast, but he still felt the pain. It gave him pause, but not for long, and he quickly fired back, hitting the Trid in the knee.

The alien dropped to one knee but continued shooting, apparently determined to take Fletcher's life at any cost.

Another shot struck Fletcher in the chest, and this time the pain was so strong it made him scream. He felt the pain in his torso like a throbbing heat wave, spreading through his limbs, and he fought it with everything he had. Fletcher lifted the rifle, his hands shaking as he aimed, and together the two enemies fired a final time.

As he fired something slammed into Fletcher's side, knocking him against the wall and out of the enemy's line of sight. It was Nona, just in the nick of time, having blocked the shot with her own arm. She lingered on him for a moment, wrapping her arms around the man. "W-What just happened?" muttered Fletcher, pulling back to see the woman's face.

She looked down at him, a strained look on her face. "Sorry, sir," said Nona. "I had to do something."

There was blood coming from her shoulder. "God-dammit," said Fletcher, leaning closer to check on Nona's wound. "You're hurt!"

"I-I'm fine," she answered. "Just a scrape. It didn't break the seal in the second layer."

He nodded, slowly, then looked at the Trid that had attacked him. The alien was sitting motionless, still on its knees with its head leaned back. The bullet had penetrated its forehead, from what he could tell.

A clean kill, quick and easy.

Thank God, thought Fletcher, looking behind the woman who saved him. The rest of his team had already finished up the remaining enemy soldiers. They were all still alive, everyone in one piece.

He stood, reaching down to Nona. "Are you ready to keep going?" he asked.

She smiled, giving him a quick nod, then grasped his hand with hers. "To the job, sir."

Alpha-line Q-Ship, Paladin System

Lars' mind had drifted as he held his position, watching *Unsurpassed* at a safe distance. The Black Eagles around him, mesmerizing him with their steady hovering. That's why he had to blink to clear his vision when a string of Sting Rays departed from *Unsurpassed*, heading in the direction of Onyx station.

"This is Carnivore," Lars said over the comms. "We have enemy activity. Let's show those giant fish that they need to back up."

"Yes, Lieutenant," said one of the other pilots.

"Lone Wolf and Escrema, I want you two to bait *Unsurpassed*," ordered Lars. "Draw that baby away from their current location."

They agreed wholeheartedly. Besides Lars, they were the only two pilots flying Q-Ships, which stood a chance of taunting the giant battleship. It was an ineffective assault attempt, but it was definitely going to work to distract *Unsurpassed.*

Lars, happy to finally have some action, activated the thrusters, speeding forward, ahead of the Black Eagles and cloaked. He sprayed a round of bullets at the first Sting Rays, which took them off guard. They were probably readying their attack for the line of Black Eagles in the distance, not realizing anyone was that close.

They reacted at once, launching their own attacks blindly in front of them.

"Whoa now ugly fish," hollered Lars. "Shouldn't you know what you're firing at before blindly shooting?"

"Big heads and small brains," sang Lone Wolf.

Lars spun the Q-Ship around, darting out of the line of fire of the Black Eagles behind him. Taking advantage of his cloak he fired at the under bellies of the Sting Rays, taking two of the closest ones out.

"Oh shit," yelled Trapeze. "I've been hit."

Lars' eyes darted to his radar and spotted the Black Eagle slow, falling out of position. "Get out of here!"

"Copy that," said the pilot breathlessly.

Having the element of surprise had been in their favor, Lars realized as they picked the Stingrays off one by one.

"*Unsurpassed* is launching missiles," yelled Escrema, her tone urgent.

"Sounds like you're doing your job and pissing them off," said Lars, watching the missile on the radar. It swerved, heading in the direction of Escrema's ship. The Q-Ship sped in the opposite direction, giving the weapon a chase to impress. Unexpectedly the missile changed direction, heading straight in the direction of the Black Eagles.

"Black Eagles!" yelled Lars. "Break formation. Missile headed your way."

The attack on the Sting Rays halted as all of the Black Eagles darted in different directions, making the missile choose a new target. Lars sped the Q-Ship in the direction of the missile chasing after it. The Black Eagles weren't in the clear yet, not at all.

"Two more missiles have been deployed," yelled Lone Wolf.

"Damn it!" yelled Lars. "Get after those. And Black Eagles follow after the Stingrays. They are again headed for Onyx station."

Lars tried to lock onto the missile, but each time he had it in his sights the fucker changed directions. It turned abruptly, doing a one-eighty and speeding at him.

"Way to make it easy on me," he said, firing at the missile...but the button stuck. *It was fucking stuck.* Lars tried again, but it still didn't work. There was something wrong.

"Get out of there or blow it up, Carnivore," yelled Lone Wolf.

"I'm trying, but there's a malfunction with the ammunition," said Lars. The warning sensor began blaring, alerting him he was about to be hit. He activated the thrusters, speeding away at once. It was too late though. The missile collided into the side of the Q-Ship, knocking Lars so hard he felt his teeth shaking in his mouth.

Upper Deck. Onyx Station, Paladin System

Fletcher slammed one of the larger Trids against the wall and pinned his weird-ass three-fingered hands behind his back.

"Hey, that hurts," muttered the Trid, eating the wall as Fletcher had intended.

"Too fucking bad," said Fletcher, nodding as Nona pushed a pirate past them. They were lined up down the corridor. It was one of the biggest busts that had happened under the Federation's nose. With these assholes put away, there might be a bit more peace. Well, until more scum replaced them. It was always a repeating cycle.

Fletcher wasn't cynical. He was realistic. There was a balance, and the only way it was achieved was if good had evil to go after.

He'd been all over the galaxy and had always found a villain to fight, even when he wasn't looking for one.

His father had taught him everything he knew, and his words often chimed in his head—especially at a time like this, when victory had been achieved. "Son, the good people weren't put here to keep evil in check. Evil was put here to remind us that there's a reason we fight. It's to protect what we should value most: Life. Life itself is the greatest treasure."

Fletcher shoved the pirate hard into the wall before pulling him back and marching him into line with the others.

Alpha-line Q-Ship, Paladin System

"I've been hit," yelled Lars. Warning lights flashed on his dashboard. The fact that he'd taken a serious hit on his armor wasn't what was most alarming to him in that moment. It was the fact of what was on the radar.

"There's another missile on your tail," yelled Lone Wolf.

Lars could take one hit, but probably not a second.

"You got to get out of there," said Escrema.

"We're coming after you," said Lone Wolf.

"You stay to the plan," said Lars, attempting to quickly regain composure after being rocked hard. "Your mission is *Unsurpassed*."

"Yes sir," answered Lone Wolf, although he sounded reluctant.

Lars couldn't shoot down the missile. That was clear enough. There was another option though, he thought. There's another one besides simply running. He knew that, but it was like remembering a dream from the night before. It was there and not.

The Black Eagles had done as he requested and were fending off the Sting Rays. They nearly had them cornered, which would mean their surrender was soon. Lone Wolf and Escrema were keeping *Unsurpassed* mostly occupied. And luckily one of them had been able to shoot down the other missile. But one missile was hot on Lars' ass.

It's not going to quit until it hits its target, he thought, swerving from side to side, trying to keep as much distance as possible between his ship and the missile. All at once, like a dream popping into one's mind randomly, Lars remembered one of the best perks of the Q-Ship. They looked like transport ships, but were much sleeker in their pure form. And while being faster would offer a benefit as far as keeping away from the missile, it wasn't going to be what actually saved his ass completely.

Lars slowed the Q-Ship, which he realized was a deadly move. It was the only way though.

"What are you doing Carnivore?" asked Lone Wolf. "You're about to get hit again."

"I know, but I've got to try this," said Lars. He hit the button to unlatch the outer armor, but stayed in place for a long moment. The missile was almost about to hit. Lars readied both thrusters, but didn't move. The timing had to be perfect. The missile was dangerously close. Lars closed his eyes and did something he hadn't done in a long time. He prayed. *Please let this work.*

Lars' eyes popped open and he pushed the controls forward just before the missile hit. The Q-Ship dropped its armor and sped forward at break neck speed. The armor left behind hovered in space for a moment and then *bam!* The impact pushed Lars forward again. But he wasn't hit because the armor he shed took the attack.

Upper Deck, Onyx Station, Paladin System

Eddie set Julianna against the wall in the safe room, although she immediately slid down. She was completely unconscious, but safe for now...or so it seemed. Eddie could hear a commotion in the distance. They had strayed from the plan, but it wasn't too late to recover. Maybe Felix had taken the bait. He would have assumed that the general had been shot with the degen. There were so many things that could have gone wrong. For instance, the real general could be infected. Eddie pushed that thought out of his mind as he propped Julianna up again. She kept sliding down, since her muscles were limp from the antidote.

"General, your time has come," said an icy voice at Eddie's back. "Or rather, your time is up."

Eddie's back tensed. From the rear, he no doubt looked like the general. It had worked, but he couldn't allow himself a moment to rejoice.

His fingers twitched at his side.

"Don't even think about it. Hands up," said Felix. His voice was rusty, like the way a saw sounds when cutting metal. "Just turn around and prepare to die like a man."

Holding up his hands, Eddie took in a steadying breath. "If you wanted me dead…" he began, making his voice a course whisper, so it wasn't easily discernable from the general's. "Why didn't you just shoot me in the head? Why infect me with the degen?"

A hostile laugh absent of any joy rattled from Felix. "Getting to you hasn't been easy. If sending a sniper after you had been an option, don't you think I would have done that long ago?"

"I'm certain you've already tried that and failed," said Eddie, his eyes on Julianna sleeping in front of him.

Another laugh. "It's true. You know that I've tried before. The explosion years ago was just the first attempt."

"When you supposedly died," said Eddie, his voice a hush.

"Yes, and then I plotted and planned for this very moment."

Julianna was defenseless, lying unconscious on the floor. She was supposed to be awake. She was supposed to be his backup. The plan was falling apart.

"And before today shooting you in the head would have been a good enough solution, but as the years ticked by I realized that wouldn't do it for me," continued Felix. "I don't just want you dead—"

"You want me to suffer," said Eddie, his attention still on Julianna. He needed to move away from her. She would be a liability in her current state. And if the antidote hadn't taken full effect yet, she was still vulnerable.

"Yes, and the degen makes what was a pipedream before become a possibility," said Felix.

Eddie registered the click of a weapon a moment too late. The boom of the gun was so loud he thought it had gone off next to his ear. A searing, stabbing pain ripped through Eddie's leg, and he staggered forward. The bullet passed all the way through the side of his calf, ripping through the flesh.

Eddie yelped from the pain and surprise, catching himself on the wall behind Julianna. He tried to keep her shielded with his body, but now he was making her more of a target. Panic started to crash down on him when Eddie realized the gunshot didn't hurt as much as it should have. The nanocytes were already at work, fixing him.

Rattling, coughing laughter spilled from Felix. "Now, General, turn around so I can watch your face when I shoot you again. That must hurt like hell, since you're not enhanced. How miserable your existence will be when I leave you paralyzed. But I'll allow you to live. Isn't that nice of me?"

Eddie tested his balance on his wounded leg. Surprisingly, it had no trouble taking the pressure. He lowered his arms, readying to dart away from Julianna and grab his gun.

Another bullet ripped through his arm. The explosion was deafening. This time Eddie was more prepared and side stepped away from Julianna. He didn't stumble or let out a yelp of pain, which would only be what Felix wanted to hear.

"I believe I told you to keep your hands up, General," said Felix, his voice full of amusement. He was enjoying this too much and that fun needed to end.

Eddie cuffed his arm with his hand. It hurt like a bitch, but that's not why he was putting pressure on it.

"The thing is," began Eddie, his tone surprisingly even, having been shot twice. "I'm not the general."

Spinning around, Eddie grabbed for his gun, pulling it up in one clear motion. He fired at Felix, who stood fifteen feet away, by the entrance.

Felix moved like Julianna did—with incredibly fast reflexes.

No! Eddie thought, the realization finally hitting him. *That asshole's been enhanced!*

Felix darted away from the line of fire, keeping his own weapon up. He shot at Eddie, who was slower to respond due to his injuries. The bullet nicked at the top of his hand, making him drop his weapon.

"Who are you?" asked Felix, his voice dripping with venom. He wore a navy blue trench coat and fedora hat pulled down low over his eyes, but the severe stare was easy to read on his face.

"I'm *not* the general," said Eddie, pressing his good hand over the one that the bullet had grazed. His gun lay on the ground several feet away.

"Where is he?" asked Felix, his voice rising.

"Beats me," said Eddie with a roguish smile. "Probably watching a movie. Maybe taking a nap. He didn't seem stressed when he loaned me this suit." Eddie stared down at the suit, covered in blood in places. "It looks good on me, don't you think?"

Through clenched teeth, Felix said, "You're that waste of space that Reynolds put in charge of Ghost Squadron." His eyes fell on Julianna. "Well, you and the commander here."

The way he pointed his gun at her made Eddie feel a sudden rush of panic. This had gone from bad to worse too quickly. He had to turn things around, but currently he had three bullet wounds, no gun, and an unconscious partner. *Fucking-A!*

"Why did the general think you were competent for the job?" asked Felix, looking less flustered by the fact that he'd shot the wrong man.

"Beats me," said Eddie, taking several steps forward, making Felix tense. "Probably a momentary lapse in judgement."

A wicked grin spread over Felix's shiny face. Now that Eddie was looking at the man, he realized that his skin looked too smooth, too stretched—like he'd elected to have a great deal of plastic surgery done. "The general is a fucking idiot."

"Bullshit!" yelled Eddie. He was only five feet from the conceited monster.

"I've read through your record," taunted Felix. "You had some notable achievements. A few things that some would consider brave. But you let *them* die."

Heat flashed in Eddie's head. He knew. Knew about Eddie's parents. Demons began to pour to the surface, overwhelming him. "I didn't."

"Oh, is that right?" asked Felix, his dark eyes shining even under his wide brimmed hat. This bullying was all a part of his game. "You didn't flee?"

"I had orders," said Eddie, his lips hardly parting to let the words out. He inched forward again.

"Do you ever think what would have happened if you'd disobeyed? Would they still be alive? Maybe you *could* have saved them," said Felix, provoking him.

"I couldn't." Eddie was yelling. How did he know all this? "They were already dead. It was too late!"

"I guess you'll never be sure," said Felix flippantly. "And you went on to save an entire squadron that day, but you left your parents to die. I bet the guilt, the uncertainty, of what *could have been* just continues to eat you up inside."

Eddie launched himself forward, darting one way and then the other, avoiding the gun fire that rang out from Felix's weapon. He slammed his hand across Felix's arm, making his gun fly from his grasp. He might be enhanced, but Felix Castile wasn't trained for combat. That much was clear as soon as Eddie thrust his good leg up and slammed his foot down on Felix's.

A guttural sound echoed from Felix's mouth. He dove for the gun, but Eddie brought his fist around and slammed it into the side of his head. The assault made mention of itself in his injured arm, but it still didn't hurt like it should. Felix fell back hard on the doorframe, his ear slamming hard against the corner.

Eddie grabbed him with both hands by the jacket and then pushed his back against the wall. Felix choked on a cough. The fear was real and wild in his eyes now. Eddie couldn't stop. The insults on him had unleashed a fury he hadn't felt in a long time. Eddie spun him around, still holding him by the jacket. Felix's long finger-nailed hands grabbed for his hands but Eddie couldn't feel a thing. Only his anger. He threw Felix on the ground and was over him at once, punching him hard in the face.

The anger was overwhelming. It was all-encompassing. In the distant part of himself, he knew he needed to stop. He needed to pull back and show his humanity. But Felix's taunts played in his head, mirroring the things the demons whispered to him so often it was a waking nightmare. Felix's face flew to one side and the next. Each assault tore at Eddie making him think he could never stop. Never be good again. This man's suffering was the key to ending his own.

"Eddie," moaned a voice in the distance. Wait, no it was nearby. He paused and looked around to find Julianna groggily trying to push away from the wall. Her attempts seemed useless.

Eddie stared down at Felix. The guy's face was bloody, but his own enhancement had kept him safe enough, about like Eddie with the bullet wounds. Still, Julianna was there, awake…

Eddie looking at Julianna, remembered who he was. Remembered the things he did and the things he didn't allow himself to do. He wasn't a monster. He was a man. A good man with a good heart.

Eddie pushed himself off of Felix, who immediately groaned and covered his face with his shaking hands.

He stood over the coward for a long moment. He was weak. Too weak to fight a real fight.

"You disgust me," said Eddie, looking down at Felix. "You think you know anything about this universe? If you did, then you'd know exactly why the general picked me to lead. It's the exact reason he didn't put you on that ship to Earth."

Felix was crying. The fucking coward was crying, the one thing a man never did in battle. He had scooted back on his rear end, using his hands to propel himself toward the far wall.

Eddie shook his head. "*Honor.* The one quality that you lack over any other. At the end of the day, everything and everyone can be stolen from us. But not our integrity. And you never even had it to lose."

"I-I-I should have been able to…" cried Felix. "To go home! Don't you see what he's done to us? What they've all done? Our home world was stolen from us! I deserved to go back! I-I deserved it!"

Eddie could barely stand to look at the piece of shit before him. But he was shriveling with regrets what had already been done and couldn't be undone. It is the weak who lived in the past, feeling sorry over lives that can't be relived. *You remember your own words, Eddie,* he thought to himself.

Behind him, he heard Julianna. Eddie turned to find her pushing up from the ground. The antidote was supposed to knock her out, but the shots and the sound of the fight must have snapped her to attention. She was a real soldier through and through.

Julianna staggered for a moment, losing her balance, like she was drunk. Eddie caught her in his arms, steadying her. "Easy now," he said softly.

Her eyes fluttered like she was having trouble keeping them open. It was because of her, because of her calling out to him that he remembered who he was. That he hadn't killed Felix with his fists, although the scoundrel deserved just that. But Julianna had brought him back to himself, reminding him that one doesn't allow their enemies to make bad men of them.

"You okay?" he asked, aware of the shuffling and moaning behind him.

Julianna's eyes were unfocused but darted to something behind Eddie. They widened.

Eddie spun, putting his back to Julianna in a protective manner. Felix was still seated but now it made sense. Now, his sniveling scooting made *perfect* sense. He had pushed himself back until he was over his gun. The weapon was directed right at Eddie's head. Felix's red eyes were hinged on him, tears continuing to stream down his slick cheeks. Even so, his hand was steady as he aimed the pistol.

"This time I won't waste time shooting you in a limb," said Felix, his voice scratchy with grief. "This time I'll just shoot you directly in the head."

There was nowhere to go. Julianna had her gun, but there was no way to get to it fast enough. And Felix was so close. Too close. Eddie pushed backward, only hoping that when he was shot it gave Julianna, even in her groggy state, a chance to get her weapon ready. To shoot Felix. To save herself.

"You're completely right," said a voice. The three turned to see the general standing in the doorway, his gun held up and aimed, a hot anger in his eyes. *"This time I'll ensure you're dead."*

General Lance Reynolds shot only once. Felix fell back, hard on the ground. The bullet went straight through the center of his forehead. It was a decisive blow, quick and simple. And there could be no doubt.

Felix Castile was dead. Enhanced or not, he was gone for good.

Landing Bay, QBS *ArchAngel*, Paladin System

Julianna thought she'd never be fully awake again. She still remembered waking up to find Eddie pummeling Felix, and thinking it was a dream. More than ever before she had had to fight to stay awake. It was like trying to stay dry while stranded in the middle of a hurricane. Now the task was still excruciating, but mildly easier than before.

The light shined in Julianna's eyes, not even making her flinch.

"How do you feel?" asked Dr. Parker, lowering the penlight he'd shined at her pupils. It had been so long since Julianna had seen a doctor, or even needed to. She tried to focus on his slicked back black hair, but her eyelids drooped against her permission.

"I'm going to need you to keep your eyes open a little longer," said Dr. Parker.

Julianna widened her eyes and shook her head, trying to drive away the stubborn exhaustion. She looked at the doctor. He had black glasses that framed his slanted brown eyes.

"So again, how do you feel?" asked the doctor, showing unending patience with Julianna. She felt like they'd been at his for hours.

"Sleepy," replied Julianna.

"That's normal, considering," said Dr. Parker, lowering the pen light all the way. "Do you notice that your reflexes, speed or senses are back to normal?"

"By that do you mean my normal or regular human normal?" asked Julianna.

She noticed Eddie stir, lifting his head to look at her. He was stretched out on a cot and bandaged, although he said he really didn't need them.

"I mean *your* normal," said Dr. Parker.

Julianna stretched out one of her arms, like testing it. It was hard to feel anything over the fatigue that was blanketing her brain, wrapping snuggly around it. She opened her mouth but couldn't find an answer. How did she know if she was alright?

On the other side of the landing bay something hit the ground. Julianna swiveled her head in that direction. Hatch stood beside a damaged Q-Ship, a sort-of smile on his face. "She's fine," he called to the doctor. Then he reached out with his tentacle and picked up something tiny from the ground. He held it up and winked at her. Julianna squinted and just made out a tiny silver object. A needle. She heard the needle hit the ground.

"Thank the stars," said Eddie, throwing his head back down on the cot.

Hello, said Pip in Julianna's head. **Can you hear me?**

What? Is that you? she answered.

Oh good. You can finally hear me, said Pip in her head. **That proves that you're back to normal, whatever that is.**

Pip! A smile broke over Julianna's face. The doctor looked at her, confused.

"My AI is back," she explained.

I was here the whole time. You're the one who is back.

Right. No matter, I'm glad to hear your voice.

What? What's wrong with you? I don't show that you've experienced any brain damage.

Even Pip's teasing couldn't take the smile off of Julianna's face. They'd made it. Despite the degen and Felix and all the odds, they'd made it. And hearing Pip's voice after considering that it was gone from her head forever, was one of the biggest reliefs.

I heard that.

What?

Your current medical state has made your filter more permeable.

Do you mean you can hear the thoughts I just had?

Yes. Your attempts at blocking aren't working.

Damn it.

There was a brief pause. **Hey, Jules?**

Yes, Pip.

I miss you like a fat kid misses mac and cheese.

That's not how the phrase goes.

I'm trying something new.

It doesn't work.

Fine. Cake. I miss you like cake.

What kind of cake? asked Julianna, watching Eddie sit up. He looked as tired as she felt, but was still giving her an amused expression.

Red velvet, of course.

Why of course?

Because it's fancy.

Oh, she mused.

And red is my favorite color.

I had no idea.

Sounds like you have a newfound opportunity to get to know me better.

Maybe I will.

And a lifetime to do so.

Julianna tilted her head, bemused at the expression Eddie was giving her. He looked like he was trying to figure her out, like she was a complex equation.

"What?" she asked him just as the doctor retreated.

"What are you and Pip talking about?" he asked, testing his foot as he tried to stand.

"Cake," she said. "What's your favorite type?"

"Cheesecake," said Eddie without thinking.

The laugh popped out of Julianna's mouth, immediately making her feel more awake. "What a strange answer."

"Why is that a strange?"

She shrugged. "Just didn't expect it to be something so indulgent and rich."

"What can I say, I have expensive tastes," said Eddie.

From the other side of the landing bay, Hatch's voice cut into their conversation. "Do you know how long it will take me to install new armor on this ship?" His tentacles were waving over his head. Lars looked sideways at Knox, who seemed to be suppressing a smile.

"One to two hours," said Lars, sounding tentative.

"Just because I'm incredibly efficient doesn't mean I should have to fix your mistakes," said Hatch.

"If I didn't lose the armor then I was going to be hit by a missile," explained Lars. "What else was I supposed to do?"

"Fire at the missile!" Hatch chided.

"The guns weren't working. The button was stuck," said Lars.

"Oh. Well, that might have been my fault," said Hatch, bustling over to where Julianna and Eddie stood. "Glad you didn't die, Lars. Sorry about that."

Lars watched, a bit confused, as Hatch retreated.

"Did you really make a mistake on the guns?" asked Eddie when Hatch stopped right in front of them.

"Hell, no," said Hatch, waving a dismissive tentacle at him. "I ain't made a mistake in decades."

Julianna eyed Knox, who was already busy at work, repairing the battered Q-Ship. He was always working, never taking a break even when he looked as exhausted as she presently felt.

"It was Knox then?" asked Julianna.

Hatch looked over his shoulder at the kid before turning back. "Yes, but it's probably his first one. I would have expected a dozen more by now."

"So, you took the blame. That was nice of you," said Eddie.

"I'm not trying to be nice," said Hatch. "I'm trying to keep his morale up. An unhappy apprentice won't work as hard."

Eddie laughed. "Of course. I should have known it was something like that."

Hatch's eyes moved to something at Julianna's back. She turned to find the general quickly approaching. She saluted.

"I'm glad to see you two are up and feeling better," said Lance.

"We're fine," Julianna answered, speaking for Eddie although she hadn't meant to.

"Thank you, sir, for what you did on Onyx station," said Eddie. "Your timing couldn't have been any better."

"Actually, I could have killed Felix years ago," said Lance. "That timing would have been a *bit* better."

Eddie laughed. "Hindsight, right?"

"Precisely," said Lance. "Now, if you three wouldn't mind taking a trip with me, I have something to show you."

Unsurpassed, **Paladin System**

The ship was…

Well, it was dark. That was the best way to describe it. Eddie squinted through the blackened corridor, walking beside General Reynolds. Julianna and Hatch strode behind him.

"How did you manage to seize this ship so easily?" asked Hatch. "There's hardly any damage."

"We offered up a deal to the crew," said Lance. "Most of them were mercenaries, so there wasn't much loyalty to begin with, but with Felix dead, the crew had no incentive to keep fighting. In exchange for Unsurpassed, we offered each of them a shorter sentence. They're to spend the next year assisting in the reconstruction efforts on Kezza." He smiled, adding. "Under Federationship supervision, of course."

The corridors were spacious and from everything Eddie could tell the ship was incredibly well made. Lance turned when they were on the bridge. "Hatch, what do you make of this ship?"

Hatch appraised the area, squinting too from the darkness. "It's got potential, although lacking many of the Federation conveniences that we're all used to."

The general nodded, his hands behind his back. "But that's something that we can fix with time."

"Fix?" asked Julianna. "Do you mean this ship, *Unsurpassed* is ours?"

The general nodded. "That's why I ordered you not to demolish it in battle. As I mentioned before, I need *Arch-Angel* back for other business. *Unsurpassed* is more than enough to hold Ghost Squadron, with room to grow. It's powerful, strong, equipped and I'm prepared to give you the resources you need to upgrade it."

Eddie stared around at the darkened bridge. It was a beautiful ship. And with Hatch's help, it would be even better. More importantly, it would be *their* ship, his and Julianna's. Something they could put their mark on and truly own.

"However, I don't like the name *Unsurpassed*," said Lance, grimacing. "It brings up bad feelings connected to a bad man."

"Yeah, I agree," said Julianna, thinking. "We'll have to figure out something else."

Lance held up a single finger, pointing toward the ceiling. "I think I might have a solution for you." The lights on the bridge all came to life, making the space suddenly bright. Monitors all around the area flickered with activity. The strategy table in the middle of the space lit up blue, showing their present location. The whole bridge took on a new, vibrant life.

"I called an old friend," began Lance, "and he agreed to help us out. I think you've all met. Please say hello to your new ship, Ricky Bobby."

Julianna's mouth popped open. Surprise mingled with pure joy sprang to her face. "Ricky Bobby! You're here?"

"Hello, Julianna. It's good to see you again," said her old AI. "I'm ready for our next adventure."

EPILOGUE

Jaslene Corporation, Federation Border Station Seven

Penrae straightened the collar of her crisp blouse in the reflection of the glass doors. Wearing tightly fitting clothes always took getting used to for her. Well, wearing clothes in general, really. It was a necessary evil, though.

She eyed the image that stared back at her. Her hair was platinum blonde and curled tightly under at the ends, like a famous female who had once lived on Earth. Penrae thought for a moment. Marilyn something…

She shook off the thought, realizing she'd been staring at her image for a whole minute. That would raise suspicions, which could ruin everything. Verdok was counting on her. The council and the elders had entrusted her with this task—her first big mission.

When she swallowed to combat her nervousness, she noticed how strange her throat felt. The bones and cartilage produced a strange sensation as they moved.

Focus, Penrae told herself, striding forward.

A male dressed in a uniform opened the door for her when she was near the office's entrance.

"Good morning, Ms. Jaslene," the doorman said with a sensitive smile. "What did you think of the game last night?"

Penrae cleared her throat and tried to smile. It was such a weird sensation that she wasn't familiar with yet. Verdok said she'd get used to this and faster with each time. She hoped he was right. "I thought it was great," she remarked, bustling through the open door.

The man's smile fell. "Oh, but the Comets lost. I thought you owned the team?"

Penrae straightened. Tensed. She turned to face him directly, reading his nametag ever so briefly. "Charles, you know I don't care about winning and losing. I enjoy the sport of it all."

The grin returned to Charles' face, this time wider. "That's the spirit Ms. Jaslene. We could all learn something from you."

Penrae gave a curt nod and turned back for the elevators. *That was close. Too close.* She replayed Verdok's words in her head. "Keep it brief. The less you say and do, the better."

The elevator was empty and for that Penrae was grateful. She held her briefcase close to her body, which was slender and curvaceous. Peering down, she chanced a glance at her chest. Boobs were such a bizarre thing that humans had. And this one had a full pair that made her small waist even more accentuated.

However, she was grateful that the CEO of Jaslene Corporation had been a female. That was how Penrae had landed this mission. It wouldn't be impossible for a male to pull off this role, but it would have been an unnecessary risk. It took less time for Penrae to adapt to a female human's body, due there being a partial overlap in certain biological functions. Had she been required to perform the part of a male, it would have take more time to fully acclimate herself to the role.

The doors slid open when the elevator arrived at the main floor. A female with auburn hair and round glasses gazed up from her desk. She glanced back down absentmindedly and then took a second look at Penrae, startled.

"Ms. Jaslene," stammered the female, standing and hurrying around the desk. "I didn't know you were coming in today. You usually take Wednesdays off."

Penrae cleared her throat and kept her chin high. "I just had a last-minute affair to deal with."

"Is it the Murphy account?" asked the female, her voice high-pitched with nervousness. "I assured you I'd deal with it. Everything is fine now, I promise."

"No, it's not the Murphy case," said Penrae, her voice clear and deliberate. She strode for the door on the other side of the office—the one marked "Mary Jaslene, CEO."

"Oh. Well, is there something I could take care of for you?" asked the female, trailing behind Penrae. "I know you prefer to spend this day with your family, and I'm happy to—"

Penrae swung around, her movements graceful. It was the same way she'd seen the real Mary Jaslene walk when she'd encountered her that morning. "I do prefer to spend this time away from the office, so please leave me to my work. I won't need anything from you."

The female smoothed her pencil skirt, looking flustered. "Okay, then I'll just go back to…" There was a strange look in the receptionist's eyes like she was caught off guard by how the CEO was acting.

Penrae smiled serenely at the woman, making her face soften. "Thank you. I've made a small error with one of the accounts and just want to fix it before it is noticed. You shouldn't worry about it since it's my blunder. And let's keep it a secret, okay?"

The female's hesitation vanished. Her face broke with relief. "Of course. I thought you were double checking my work. Don't worry, no one will hear about this from me."

"I trust your work implicitly, and that you'll keep this in confidence," said Penrae and then headed for the door at the end of the room. She strode across the space, taking each step carefully in the high heels. They were such an odd thing to wear, and her nervousness made her think she'd trip and fall on her face. That's definitely not something the poised CEO of Jaslene Corporation would do.

Penrae didn't let out a breath until she was inside the expansive office. It was set up exactly as Hendrix had said it would be, which meant that the safe was on the back wall behind the painting of a bird.

All Penrae had to do was input the code and then she'd have what she came for. It was only a stack of papers, but those papers held the key. The Federation was hiding the Tangle Thief, and Penrae was going to help find it. Once the council was in possession of it, then they'd be unstoppable.

Knowing she only had one chance to disable the safe before the alarm was triggered, Penrae reverted to her natural form. She slid across the carpet, her scales leaving behind flakes in the fibers. Shedding season was nearing and soon Penrae would have a new skin, more iridescent than the one before.

She slithered to the painting, catching her image in the mirror sitting on the CEO's desk. The female apparently looked into a mirror when talking on the phone to ensure she always smiled when she spoke. Penrae had learned this about the CEO when preparing for this mission. Her red serpent face with its large green eyes stared back at her. The Saverus species didn't smile, which was why she'd practiced the gesture.

The giant snake turned her attention to the painting on the wall, her small arms extending in the direction of the vault. This had all gone to plan, and soon she'd have the praise of the council. Soon they'd be that much closer to taking anything they so desired.

Penrae's forked tongue slipped from her mouth with a gentle hiss, a gesture reeking of her elation. The Saverus might be limited in their expressions, but the living forms they could shapeshift into were endless. Who needed to smile when they could steal the appearance of anyone in the universe?

FINIS

AUTHOR NOTES - SARAH NOFFKE

JANUARY 19, 2018

After the last author notes, I feel like there's a precedent set. And (aka Anderle) is all expecting me to pick up the mic in these notes and wax about how cray-cray he is and throw shade on him, prompting him to reply. However, I cordially decline to partake in such affairs at this junction.

No, I do not leave the house very often. And yes, I talk to myself. Well, I'm talking to my cat most of the time, if I'm honest. But he speaks Catenese, which I haven't mastered, as of yet, and therefore I understand little of his replies.

Closing out this arc was a real challenge. As authors, we're faced with upping the ante, but not so much that we can't reach the bar in the next book. I came up with what I thought was a perfect ending for this book: Assassinate General Reynolds. Okay, not really, that was just the premise for the book. I tend to hash out these ideas late at night. I know I'll suffer in the morning, but that's when the wall comes down and I get those "Whoa" ideas.

I love to play around with my author notes, but in all seriousness, working with And is really great. No matter what hairball of an idea I've brought to him, he's always entertained it and tried to make it work. So just imagine when I approached him about this book. "I want to create a drug that undoes nanos entirely." And (Michael) totally entertained the idea and helped us to flush it out until we had something that worked. I'll admit that I started to craft a backup plan, thinking that I'd gone too far. However, the awesome thing about TKG is that anything is possible, but within certain perimeters.

On an unrelated note. Is the And nickname confusing to anyone else? I don't think it's going to stick.

Onto more important business. The crew in this book didn't get as sloshed this time thanks to nanos making that buzz a little harder to obtain. So please note, don't upgrade me unless absolutely necessary. Eddie and Julianna did enjoy a few shots of Greek Pirate, which we can thank reader Charles Wood for that idea. And thank you to Micky Cocker who pretty much named most of the characters in this book. Her awesome efforts are helping us not to repeat names from other TKG series. Love getting the suggestions on drinks, characters and locations, so please keep sending them. Join the Facebook fan group. We post often and there's always tons of fun interaction. Naming characters, drinks and planets is hard. I need your help.

Here's a little insider. I named the pilots and ground forces soldiers after characters from my other series outside of TKG. Some would call that lazy, but I call it inserting Easter Eggs for my most loyal fans. Some are actual names of characters like Nona. And some are just references to important characters like Lone Wolf, Trapeze and Escrema.

Anyway, thanks for all the support for this series. The adventures will continue in book five, if for no other reason than to give me an opportunity to call my cowriter funny names.

Sarah

First, let me say THANK YOU for not only reading this story, but all the way past Noff's author notes, as well.

Since Sarah threw down the gauntlet, I won't comment on her author notes except to say the term 'catonese' (which I originally misread to be 'cantonese' and did a double take) is priceless!

And 'And' has to go, may it be but a blip in the history of Author Notes. Maybe one of those game show host scenarios where we have our fan on stage, the announcer speaking to a hush audience, "And for EXTRA Points, can YOU name the nickname Sarah Noffke gave Michael that lasted all of one book? For Extra *EXTRA* points, can you NAME the book?"

Tick tock…tick tock…tick tock… "And and Degeneration?" the contestant replies.

<Pregnant pause while the game show host looks down at his answer card, up to the contestant a frown on his face. He looks back down at his card, slowly shaking his head

before his eyes LIGHT up and he *WOOOPS* YOU ARE CORRECT!>

WOOHOOO!

So, in order for this fabrication to ever have a chance to come true, Sarah can't do that to me again.

Just saying.

THANK YOU SARAH for playing in the Kurtherian Universe. We the fans are the richer in our lives for your characters, for your fun, and for your stories ;-)

Sarah also has a huge set of wonderful stories herself. You should check them out when you are ready for something a bit different, and yet with author's you already know.

For Sarah – check out her website here: http://www.sarahnoffke.com

And thank you Sarah. I'm usually not good with accepting compliments (not that I didn't crave them like a kid wants sugar when younger, a teenage boy wants that girl to say 'hi' and a man wants that car he can't afford) but when it happens?

I'm secretly happy, but stutter over the acceptance.

Kind of like now.

Damn!

;-)

Ad Aeternitatem,

Michael

ACKNOWLEDGMENTS

SARAH NOFFKE

Thank you to Michael Anderle for taking my calls and allowing me to play in this universe. It's been a blast since the beginning.

Thank you to Craig Martelle for cheering for me. I've learned so much working with you. This wild ride just keeps going and going.

Thank you to Jen, Tim, Steve, Andrew and Jeff for all the work on the books, covers and championing so much of the publishing.

Thank you to our beta team. I can't believe how fast you all can turn around books. The JIT team sometimes scares me, but usually just with how impressively knowledgeable they are.

Thank you to our amazing readers. I asked myself a question the other day and it had a strange answer. I asked if I would still write if trapped on a desert island and no one would ever read the books. The answer was yes, but the feeling connected to it was different. It wouldn't be as much fun to write if there wasn't awesome readers to share it with. Thank you.

Thank you to my friends and family for all the support and love.

THE GHOST SQUADRON

by Sarah Noffke and Michael Anderle

Formation (01)

Exploration (02)

Evolution (03)

Degeneration (04)

Impersonation (05)

Recollection (06)

WANT MORE?

ENTER

THE KURTHERIAN GAMBIT UNIVERSE

A desperate move by a dying alien race transforms the unknown world into an ever-expanding, paranormal, intergalactic force.

The Kurtherian Gambit Universe contains more than 100 titles in series created by Michael Anderle and many talented co-authors. For a complete list of books in this phenomenal marriage of paranormal and science fiction, go to:

http://kurtherianbooks.com/timeline-kurtherian/

ABOUT SARAH NOFFKE

Sarah Noffke, an Amazon Best Seller, writes YA and NA sci-fi fantasy, paranormal and urban fantasy. She is the author of the Lucidites, Reverians, Ren, Vagabond Circus, Olento Research and Soul Stone Mage series. Noffke holds a Masters of Management and teaches college business courses. Most of her students have no idea that she toils away her hours crafting fictional characters. Noffke's books are top rated and best-sellers on Kindle. Currently, she has eighteen novels published. Her books are available in paperback, audio and in Spanish, Portuguese and Italian.

SARAH NOFFKE SOCIAL

Website: http://www.sarahnoffke.com
Facebook: https://www.facebook.com/officialsarahnoffke
Amazon: http://amzn.to/1JGQjRn

THE SOUL STONE MAGE SERIES

House of Enchanted #1

The Kingdom of Virgo has lived in peace for thousands of years…until now.

The humans from Terran have always been real assholes to the witches of Virgo. Now a silent war is brewing, and the timing couldn't be worse. Princess Azure will soon be crowned queen of the Kingdom of Virgo.

In the Dark Forest a powerful potion-maker has been murdered.

Charmsgood was the only wizard who could stop a deadly virus plaguing Virgo. He also knew about the devastation the people from Terran had done to the forest.

Azure must protect her people. Mend the Dark Forest. Create alliances with savage beasts. No biggie, right?

But on coronation day everything changes. Princess Azure isn't who she thought she was and that's a big freaking problem.

Welcome to The Revelations of Oriceran.

The Dark Forest #2

Mountain of Truth #3

Land of Terran #4

New Egypt #5

Lancothy #6

a psychic power. Desperate to do whatever it takes to earn her gift, she endures painful daily injections along with commands from her overbearing, loveless father. One of the few bright spots in her life is the return of a friend she had thought dead—but with his return comes the knowledge of a shocking, unforgivable truth. The society Em thought was protecting her has actually been betraying her, but she has no idea how to break away from its authority without hurting everyone she loves.

<u>Rebels, #2</u>

<u>Warriors, #3</u>

VAGABOND CIRCUS SERIES

<u>Suspended, #1</u>

When a stranger joins the cast of Vagabond Circus—a circus that is run by Dream Travelers and features real magic—mysterious events start happening. The once orderly grounds of the circus become riddled with hidden threats. And the ringmaster realizes not only are his circus and its magic at risk, but also his very life.

Vagabond Circus caters to the skeptics. Without skeptics, it would close its doors. This is because Vagabond Circus runs for two reasons and only two reasons: first and foremost to provide the lost and lonely Dream Travelers a place to be illustrious. And secondly, to show the nonbelievers that there's still magic in the world. If they believe, then they care, and if they care, then they don't destroy. They stop the small abuse that day-by-day breaks down humanity's spirit. If Vagabond Circus makes one skeptic believe in magic, then they halt the cycle, just a little bit. They allow a little more love into this world. That's Dr. Dave Raydon's mission. And that's why this ringmaster recruits. That's why he directs. That's why he puts on a show that makes people question their beliefs. He wants the world to believe in magic once again.

<u>Paralyzed, #2</u>

<u>Released, #3</u>

<u>Ren: The Man Behind the Monster, #1</u>

Born with the power to control minds, hypnotize others, and read thoughts, Ren Lewis, is certain of one thing: God made a mistake. No one should be born with so much power. A monster awoke in him the same year he received his gifts. At ten years old. A prepubescent boy with the ability to control others might merely abuse his powers, but Ren allowed it to corrupt him. And since he can have and do anything he wants, Ren should be happy. However, his journey teaches him that harboring so much power doesn't bring happiness, it steals it. Once this realization sets in, Ren makes up his mind to do the one thing that can bring his tortured soul some peace. He must kill the monster.

Note This book is NA and has strong language, violence and sexual references.

<u>Ren: God's Little Monster, #2</u>

<u>Ren: The Monster Inside the Monster, #3</u>

<u>Ren: The Monster's Adventure, #3.5</u>

<u>Ren: The Monster's Death, #4</u>